THE LITTLE MERMAID
(A HORROR STORY)

THE LITTLE MERMAID

(A HORROR STORY)

J. BOYETT

SALTIMBANQUE BOOKS

NEW YORK

For Pam Carter, Dawn Drinkwater, and Andy Shanks.

Table of Contents

THE LITTLE MERMAID
(A HORROR STORY)

One

The sky, a ceramic blue bowl. Brenna drives her sputtering hatchback through Long Beach. Parks at the two-story beachfront house; gets out of the car, takes in the house through her five-dollar sunglasses.

Maybe Mark's around back, in the water.... But no, she sees him now, stepping out onto the porch, shirtless in his swimming trunks. They both smile. Brenna walks to the porch. She holds up the copy of the New York *Post* as she approaches.

"My hero," she says, half-ironically. Only half. He really is a hero, after all.

He almost winces. "Come on," he says.

"You are," she insists mildly, and tilts her head back, inviting him to give her a kiss. They exchange a peck.

She puts her palm against his chest for a moment, to let him know she really is proud of him. After that, since he doesn't want her to make a big deal, she drops it.

They turn back to the house, owned by clients of Mark's. He's house-sitting. "Nice," she says.

"Yup," says Mark. "George and Albert left a note telling me to feel free to throw some wild parties. But I assume they were kidding."

"Do you want to throw a wild party?"

"No."

"How funny," says Brenna, as they walk up the porch steps, "being rich enough to take a European vacation from your summer home in Long Beach." She says it without envy. Merely an amusing anthropological item.

Inside, Mark gives her the tour. It's tasteful and comfortable. Probably George and Albert think it has a hint of a rustic feel. Somehow it's darker than you'd expect, even with the gorgeous day, even with the window open. Like it's in the shade. What's the point of a beach house that doesn't let in the light, Brenna wonders? But it's a nice place. Wonderful, to be right on the water.

He takes her upstairs and they stand on the threshold of the bedroom. Mark nods at the bed. "That's where the action is gonna happen," he says, and she laughs.

Back downstairs, Mark nods at the newspaper still in her hand, the one with the picture of him and the story about how he saved the little boy from drowning the other day. "Get rid of that thing," he says, embarrassed again. Brenna steps into the kitchen and places it in the wastebasket.

They go out the back door and look out at the surf. They seem like people accustomed to the beach, with their tans and fit physiques, Brenna in loose shorts and T-shirt over her bathing suit, the sculpted triangle of Mark's torso rising out of his. But they have an angular, New-York edge. Dark-haired Brenna is beautiful but not the sort of face you see on magazines. A very well-kept forty, she's a few years older than Mark. She looks at everything from an amused distance, not in an unkind way; though the irony dissipates as she takes off her sunglasses and gazes at the sea.

Holly's coming in from Philly in a couple hours to spend a few nights, Mark asks again if Brenna will stay over. She says no, conveying by her tone that she dislikes repeating herself.

Mark knows that, and there's a hint of apology in his own voice. But also frustration. "Everything would go more smoothly if you were here."

"Not for me. I need to get some painting done. And I have to teach yoga. It's already a big commute from Coney Island up to Union Square. How am I supposed to manage it from Long Beach?"

"You're not teaching tomorrow, though."

"I picked up a class, actually. Besides, I have to paint." Mark nods in recognition, looks out at the water again. Brenna chides him: "I know it's awkward. But you didn't have to invite her over, you know."

"She kind of invited herself."

"You didn't have to let her do that, either."

"I know. It's my responsibility. She just sounded so sad." Holly works as a lighting designer for a university's theater department. Mark's explained to Brenna that it's Holly's first summer break since moving to Philadelphia, and she's at loose ends. Nowhere to go.

"Well," says Brenna. "Maybe it's true that she's your responsibility. That's for you to judge. But she isn't mine. Anyway, I don't think she'll be less sad after a week of making passes at you and you brushing her off."

"That's why it would be nice if you were here, because then she wouldn't try anything." Brenna's face puckers with its first grimace of true irritation. Seeing that, Mark raises his arms in surrender: "But you can't stay. I respect that. I'll be a big boy, promise. And like you say, I could have told her not to come. I just didn't feel like I could, was all."

She gives his muscular ass a firm squeeze and kisses him on the shoulder. "Stick to rescuing drowning little boys," she says. "It's easier than rescuing lovelorn one-night stands from five years ago."

Brenna leaves her shirt and shorts on the back porch and rubs suntan lotion on her body. They go play in the ocean. Brenna swims till she's tired. Then she frolics with Mark. Then she swims some more. It's hard to tell how much time passes.

She swims back to Mark and kisses him, says "I love you," he says "I love you too." She trudges through the drag of the surf back to the shore. Once she's halfway between the sea and the house she turns around. Mark's watching her, he waves. She waves back. The crashing of the waves subsumes everything, so that even though she can hear the traffic passing in front of the house it seems as if it's far away, as if the noise of the surf were elbowing the mundane sound out of the universe, or out toward its periphery.

Without bothering about a towel, Brenna lays on the sand, not caring that it cakes her body. She'll take a shower before she goes home. If she can't get the sand out of her bathing suit she'll just go home with nothing on under her shorts.

She closes her eyes. It's getting late in the afternoon—the sunlight bears down on her like something with real mass, but it's cooler than it was and it's not an uncomfortably strong pressure, more like a firm weight.

After a while she's half-dozing. Again, no track of time. She tells herself that she had better open her eyes, rouse herself, sit up. That suntan lotion won't keep her from getting fried.

The effort required to sit up and open her eyes is brutal. She squints into the sea and has to look away. Even though the light is getting gentler, the sun is at just the right angle for shards of sunlight to bounce back off the wavelets at her.

She forces herself to look into the water again, because she wants to locate Mark. Not that she's worried about him; he's a lifeguard. Still, she wants to see him.

She finds him. He's swimming, strongly and happily, oblivious to all else, she supposes. Now that she knows he's all right, she's surprised not to feel at ease again.... She's still not sure why she felt uneasy for him in the first place....

Pale flash—there's a thing in the water. Some strange thing, an artifact, a piece of trash. No, she realizes with alarm, standing up: a creature, some animal, there in the water with Mark.

As she's about to cry for him to look out, get out of the water, she blinks and squints again. Oh; it's only a girl. Why couldn't she tell that at first?

Why did she think for an instant that it was something other than a girl?

The new swimmer isn't so far out that Brenna can't make out a flash of nipple. Skinny-dipping. Why not. Probably the girl lives around here. She's young, why not go skinny-dipping.

But as Brenna stares at the girl's face she realizes she looks dazed, shocked. Like she suddenly woke up in the middle of the ocean and doesn't know how to swim. A wave crashes over her head. When her open-mouthed face drifts up again, it's tilted back, seawater drizzling out from between her lips, eyes rolling back.

"Mark!" shouts Brenna. He can't hear her. She runs to the surf, tearing the lining of her throat, shouting, "Mark! Mark!"

He hears, looks back to shore at her. She points to the drowning girl. Mark looks over, sees her. Plunges to her across the water.

Brenna stops shouting and only watches. Nothing she can do now, not anything better than what Mark can do. He'll be pulling the girl ashore before Brenna could ever reach her. Now that everything is out of her hands, the adrenaline subsides and she has the chance to wonder: what made her think she could make out the drowning girl's expressions so clearly? She's too far away for that. It wouldn't be possible.

Two

The cops listen to Mark, frowning. Brenna and Holly hang back, leaning against the wall, letting Mark handle this. It's his deal.

The waif blinks up innocently at them, covered now with Mark's T-shirt. She doesn't like tearing her eyes from Mark, at whom she beams. Only when Mark indicates that she should pay attention to the policemen, gesturing towards them and gently saying "Go on, go on," only then will she consent to listen to their questions.

She won't speak. Can she tell them her name, the cops ask?

She shakes her head.

Does she know her name?

She nods.

But she can't tell them what it is. Is she mute?

She nods.

Okay, so she's mute. Mark helpfully brings a notepad and a pen from the kitchen counter. One of the cops slides it in front of the waif. It's impossible to get her to pay attention to it until Mark intervenes, gently but firmly pointing at it.

Keeping his patience, the policeman asks if she can write her name.

The waif shakes her head.

She can't write her name. Can she write?

She shakes her head.

She can't write. Is she illiterate?

The waif nods. The other cop, the one not talking, standing to the side with his arms folded, rolls his eyes.

Brenna nudges Holly—it's too crowded, they're stifling Mark's and the policemen's efforts. She feels like a spectator. It's a job for the cops, and for Mark, who seems to have been deputized by circumstances. Brenna gets a vibe that Holly resents having to leave. Maybe it's because she wants to stick around and watch the mystery play out, but Brenna knows that mainly it's because Holly, like the waif, would prefer to stay close to Mark.

Once out on the porch, Holly lights a cigarette, cupping the flame against the breeze. With her brown ponytail and her mildly ironic eyeglasses, Holly is a pretty woman who doesn't particularly think of herself as such. She and Brenna aren't friends, really, but they've known each other for five years. Looking at the flame in her hands, mumbling around the cigarette in her mouth, Holly says, "So she just showed up naked in the ocean?"

The waif must have walked into the water somewhere nearby. Brenna didn't see any tracks in the sand that weren't hers or Mark's, but it isn't like she performed a thorough search. Considering her state when Mark pulled her out of the water, it's unimaginable that she could have swum a great distance. On the one hand, she wasn't exhausted enough for that. On the other, there was something wrong with her body. Now she seems fine, but when she came out of the water it was a different story.

Brenna tells how the girl's legs at first collapsed under her, once on land. At first Brenna and Mark were afraid she might be paralyzed. She wasn't, but it was like her legs had to wake up, like the waif couldn't quite control them yet. Even just now, a moment ago, in the house, the only things that seemed to fascinate her almost as much as Mark were her own legs. But not as if they're hurting her.

"Maybe something stung her," says Holly.

Brenna doesn't reply. She gazes into the sea, no longer needing to squint now that the sky is dimming. She's got to get home so she can paint in the morning, before class. It'll

10

probably be too late to paint tonight. She inhales the chemical, industrial herb of Holly's cigarette smoke.

"Something must have stung her," Holly says. "Some weird neurotoxin. Something that temporarily disabled her legs and that fucked up her brain chemistry somehow."

"Maybe," says Brenna. "A doctor should look at her." They had wondered if she was weak with hunger. But Mark had tried to bring her a cheese sandwich and it had seemed like she was going to throw up when she smelled it. Maybe she has been poisoned by something.

Already her mind is on the trek home. At least now the traffic will be light. But she prefers not to hunt for parking in Coney Island after dark. She has her pepper spray, but still.

Mark and the two cops come out. Brenna is surprised that the waif isn't with them. As she listens to them talk she realizes that the cops are leaving the waif here, with Mark, in George's and Albert's house.

They aren't happy about it—that is, the talker isn't, the one who has taken an interest. He can't see what other option they have. Other than being mute, there doesn't seem to be anything wrong with her. She seems too well-groomed and healthy to be a young homeless vagrant—too generally undamaged. Nobody in the area has reported a missing person. She plainly wants to be with Mark.

The cop's eyes drift over to Brenna as he talks to Mark. She realizes that he is counting on her feminine influence to deter Mark from taking advantage of the waif. Brenna's tempted to set the cop straight, let him know she's not staying here. But what would be the point? She's annoyed, but it's not her business. Besides, it's not as if Brenna thinks Mark is going to rape the waif.

Still, she does go so far as to say, "Holly thinks maybe she was stung by something. Maybe we should take her to the emergency room."

The cop looks at her mournfully. "I asked her if something stung her, she shook her head no. Far as I can tell, she's lucid.

A lucid, illiterate mute. I can't run her in for being weird."

The cops leave. Brenna says to Holly and Mark, "I have to go, too. I've already stayed later than I planned."

Holly looks surprised. Mark says, "Hang on. Can I talk to you for a second?"

Goddammit. She knew he was going to try to talk her into sticking around. He follows her to her car. Holly politely goes back into the house and out of earshot. Mark says, "Brenna, I know you have plans tomorrow, but I could use your help with this."

"I'll make you a deal. If you need my help taking her to a hospital or a social worker or anything like that, I'll be happy to change my plans."

"I just don't see how taking her to one of those places would be appropriate. What would I tell them was wrong with her, at the hospital? She seems fine. But there's obviously something strange about her, and I can't accept kicking her out to wander the streets."

"Then you could take her to the hospital and tell them she seems fine, except that there's obviously something strange about her, and you can't accept kicking her out to wander the streets. And they can have a neurologist and psychologist examine her."

"I don't think there's anything they could do for her."

"If there's nothing they can do, then there's certainly nothing you can do."

She's got her keys out and is unlocking and opening her car door. Mark hates it when she peremptorily decides a conversation is over because she's said all she plans to say. "I think you're being selfish right now," he tells her.

Brenna pauses. Places her hand on his chest again. But says, "You take in strays, Mark. Maybe it's because you're a good person; maybe it's a neurotic compulsion. I don't know which it is, or if it's both. But it's not a thing I do."

Mark is looking around, helplessly, as if he might physically see the magic words that would convince her. "I could use some help is all, Brenna."

"If she's just a normal houseguest, then you don't need my help. If she's someone with a mental or physical problem then we should take her to a hospital because we aren't qualified to deal with that. Like I said, if you want to take her somewhere, I'm willing to help. But if you want to invite her to join you and Holly for an awkward slumber party, then that's up to you but I don't feel obligated to participate."

"You can be so infuriating sometimes."

"The reason you're having trouble arguing with me is that everything I'm saying makes sense."

"Yeah, yeah, it all makes sense. All right. Fine."

Brenna pauses, poised to sit in the car. "Mad at me?"

"Yes. No. Annoyed at you. I can be annoyed at you, and still love you."

She gives him a kiss. She won't apologize, because she's done nothing wrong. But there's something in the kiss that tries to tell him she regrets having to displease him.

She starts to get into the car. Mark takes her arm to stop her. "Hey, Brenna."

Brenna looks at him. If he keeps asking her to stay then soon she really will get mad.

She can tell that's exactly what he's going to do. But something about the confused, uneasy look in his eyes keeps her from getting angry, after all.

He shrugs, letting her see he knows it's silly but he can't help himself. "I just, I already told her she could stay. I already told her that. But now ... I feel weird about it."

She stares at him. Is he talking about a sexual thing? "Well," she says, "I trust you." She pauses to give him a chance to protest that's not what he meant, but he doesn't. "Anyway, Holly will be there." With dry amusement Brenna reflects that Holly is much more likely than herself to maintain a jealous vigilance against some young thing luring Mark into bed with her.

"I just feel weird," says Mark.

Brenna can tell that Mark's using the word "weird" as a stand-in for a whole complex of things, sensations he can't otherwise describe. Never has she seen him so discombobulated, and to tell the truth she's a little worried. If it were him alone at the house, she would break her plans and stay. But the notion of staying so she can sit making small talk with Holly and experimenting with ways to interact with the waif, both of whom are there purely because of Mark's inability to say no, sets her teeth on edge.

"I've heard your piece and you've heard mine," she says. "Do you have anything else to say? Because nothing I've heard so far will change my mind."

Mark shakes his head, but does say again, "I love you."

"I love you, too," she says, and leaves.

Three

She arrives home late, mad because it's late, too late to work. Mad at herself for being mad—she was the one who decided to stay. Lets it go, stands still and consciously relaxes till the tension melts from her body. Nothing to get mad about. The girl appeared in the surf, no one could have foreseen that. And while she felt no obligation to spend the night in Long Beach, it would have been a bit much to leave right away when Mark first had the girl on his hands.

Normally she isn't inflexible like this, childishly stamping her feet at every interruption of her plans. It's only that all day, till the waif arrived, she was looking forward to painting before bed. But fuck it. She can paint in the morning.

Brenna turns on the light and looks at her canvas as she undresses. So far she's painted a woman, nude, from behind, standing and gazing at something. The woman is not painted from life and is sparingly distorted and skillfully drawn. Having achieved some formal, technical mastery makes Brenna feel freer to paint whatever crazy things she wants, to fling paint at the canvas or roil great abstract clouds off her brush. This piece highlights her draftsmanship, almost in a show-off way. The woman whose face is turned away from the viewer and deeper into the canvas has Rubenesque proportions, and she is strangely lit.

Brenna stands naked except for socks in the cool air of the apartment, absently running her fingers over her belly. She wonders what the woman is staring at.

Now it is getting late, though, and she is tired. Her eyes are heavy from the mild sunburn she got earlier, when she dozed off. Best go to bed, trust she would be able to re-find the path tomorrow.

She begins turning off the lamps, big and small. She has heavy black-out curtains over her windows. Her apartment is a kitchen nook with a folding card table and two folding chairs; a dozen dishes and half a silverware set; a narrow cot with some sheets and one pillow; a closet with some clothes hanging and, on its floor, five pairs of shoes and a plastic container filled with underwear and socks; and lots of canvases. Brenna has been trying to figure out a cheap but safe way to put them into storage somewhere. It would also be nice to be able to afford a studio, so as not to live among the fumes. For now, she leaves the windows open all spring, summer, and most of fall, unless the weather forecast predicts rain. As she's clicking off lights she idly watches the heavy black curtains bobbing in the air. Takes a moment to listen to the street noises of traffic and shouting before tuning them out for sleep.

The lights are out. In the dark she walks to her cot. She knows exactly where it is but, to be safe, because it is dark, she steps slowly and carefully. Arriving at the cot, she lowers herself onto it and under the sheets, lying on her back in a relatively straight line.

She lies there and starts to think about the painting.

In her mind's eye she sees that strange woman her hand has conjured, gazing out on the expanse of canvas that is still hidden from Brenna. Brenna's gaze closes in on the alive but unmoving form. Soon the woman is impossibly, psychedelically close. No human woman but a primordial titan, pores like moon craters, hairs like limp tangled redwoods. Brenna progresses all the way through the back of the titan's head and now she is seeing what the titan sees, though she cannot yet make out the sights.

The control tower of her mind observes that she is in a trance. Encased in her forcefield of slight tension, each controlled breath a lungful of crackling photons, Brenna eases herself out of bed, careful not to jostle herself and break the spell. Carefully she moves through the room, turning on lights—a stubbed toe could be a flash of pain that wipes out the vision she knows she sees but can't yet access.

Carefully she prepares the paint, the brushes. Tries not to notice what she is doing.

She starts painting. There are some plans she was playing with for the rest of the canvas, clever ideas of how to render it. She tries gently to hold those plans at bay, to not even notice that she isn't noticing them.

There's a lot of blue she's using—even when she uses green it's part of a blue. Naturally it occurs to Brenna that there must be some connection with the events of the day, the ocean and all that, but she does her best not to see that thought in her mind. For fear the rationality of it will break the spell, betray her into adding a cute little fishy friend, a sinking ship symbolic of man's soul in the globalized economy, some garbage like that.

At moments it's hard for her to breathe, like her lungs are full of something. Sometimes the roar in her ears gets so loud she's scared. This is the most intense artistic experience she's ever had. She keeps painting.

The violence of her compulsion prompts her to take the canvas off the easel and put it flat on the floor. Bears down on it with her brush; naked on all fours she uses her fingers, thumbs. Panting.

A vortex she's painted, a moving swirl, a wet tunnel to another world.

All of a sudden the noise in her head is going up and up, alarming, no longer a symptom of inspiration but more like madness or a stroke. Brenna recoils from the canvas, rearing back onto her knees as she claps her hands onto her temples and lets out a cry of pain and collapses onto her side.

She lies there, hands still on her head, getting paint in her hair. The trance is gone, but it takes Brenna a moment to notice because in its place is the quivering drunkenness of exhaustion. She trembles with it, and shivers with cold because the parts of her body not patched with paint are slick with cooling sweat.

What the fuck was that?, she asks herself.

Her mind pokes gingerly through her body, probing for any aftermath to that moment of blinding pain. A stroke? She checks her mental capacity, going over her multiplication tables, silently reciting the one poem she has memorized ("Stopping By Woods On a Snowy Eve"), making sure her phone number and street address remain intact. Everything seems to check out.

She peels her hands away from her head. Better clean that quick; it's going to stain and leave her looking like a battered housewife. Oh, God, how is she going to get it out of her hair?

Though she knows she needs to get in the shower and clean herself fast, she is compelled to pause and see what she's painted.

The original woman, upon whom Brenna spent so much painstaking time, is all but obliterated, only a faint ghost drowned under the new composition. Well, that's okay. Brenna likes this new thing better. Maybe it doesn't show off her technical prowess as much—Brenna can't tell how long she spent making it, either from looking at it or from her own memory—but it has more raw power, more mystery.

And then again, the more she looks, the more she thinks it's not such a bad showcase after all. There are effects of depth, of light and shadow, so subtle that Brenna is startled she could have achieved them without consciously trying.

It has almost an Op Art quality, she thinks. As if it's moving.

As if it's a view down the throat of a whirlpool, whose suction draws you in—a whirlpool which only seems to be moving slowly because it's so far away, because between her and it there's such a long long distance for her to fall....

Brenna gasps and looks away. Skitters across the floor away from the painting, tracking oil paint across the cold linoleum.

The cold linoleum. At some point, without noticing, Brenna put slippers on her feet. But there's nothing between her bare ass and the freezing floor. Scared as she is that something is really wrong with her, she stands and walks to her shower.

Can she have some new kind of epilepsy? When she looked at her painting again it triggered something. Doesn't the idea of going into a trance or having a *petit mal* seizure because you looked at an image sound like epilepsy?

As she showers she calms herself. Simply the struggle to get oil paint out of her hair is enough to distract her. She probably does not have epilepsy. She probably did not have a stroke. At first she's uneasy at the thought that there may be some connection between the waif, who appeared to have some kind of mental trouble, and whatever just happened to her. But as she continues to think it over she decides that the two things occurring on the same day is a good sign. Her own brain suddenly, physically falling apart the day she met an eccentrically handicapped girl would be too much of a coincidence. And Brenna's never heard of any mental illness being communicable by touch. Rather than believe she caught some exotic virus from the girl, Brenna thinks it much more likely that the event, and the conversation afterwards with Mark, affected her mind more deeply and strangely than she thought.

Probably the small argument with Mark, rather than the waif. Brenna wishes her all the best, but doubts her feelings about her would be strong enough to trigger much of anything. It seems counter-intuitive that her tiny, stillborn tiff with Mark could have caused that trance, that painting, or that headache, though. Something to think about.

But not to lie awake brooding over. She has a class to teach tomorrow.

She looks at herself in the mirror and rolls her eyes, laughs at her reflection. The paint has stained. Like bruises rising through the skull from the brain.

She goes back to her cot, turning the lights off along the way. Starts to go pick up the canvas from the floor, but while she's still far away she stops short. It's like she can feel it thrumming from across the room. Once again she feels fear tickling low in her belly; not of the painting or its image, she tells herself, but of the idea there might be something wrong in her head. In the end she leaves the canvas on the floor when she turns off the last lamp. After she lays back down on her cot she remains aware of its presence.

Four

Holly doesn't like the waif and the waif does not like Holly. It's pretty plain. Holly doesn't even like being alone with the waif, because she gets a vibe like maybe the waif wouldn't stop at mere dislike. She knows that's probably just a combination of her imagination and her dislike for the girl. But it still creeps her out.

So when Mark leaves early in the morning for work, off to go safeguard the swimmers on another beach, Holly goes out to this beach alone, even though Mark made Holly promise she'd keep an eye on the waif.

Anyway, it would be depressing to hang out with the waif, even if they liked each other. The waif was inconsolable when Mark left, when he finally made her understand that, no, she really couldn't come with him. She curled up on the sofa with her head in her hands.

Actually, Holly isn't sure why Mark didn't take the waif with him. He works at a public beach, after all, it isn't as if there's restricted access. Maybe it would embarrass him to have her hanging off him all day, but he seems so worried over her that Holly's surprised he didn't opt to keep her in view.

Maybe, despite all his overblown interest and concern, a part of him really wanted to get away from the girl.

After a couple of hours of laying around and periodically slathering suntan lotion over herself, Holly decides to go in.

With trepidation she enters the house. "Hello?" she calls. No answer. Of course. Mutes don't answer.

Her bitter disappointment and jealousy at the waif's invasion humiliates her and makes her feel stupid. It isn't that she really, seriously thought that Mark would sleep with her this week, that he would come around, realize how much he'd missed her, dump Brenna. Except that, as always, a part of her did think exactly that. Her inner child, she supposes. Just enough to give the fantasy some juice.

Always, when she manages to finagle a chunk of alone-time with Mark, she knows she's setting herself up for renewed agony. There's the despair of waiting for him to make a gesture he never will, to issue an invitation that will never come; the gall of hearing him talk about Brenna, of seeing them together, the way he lights up, the way he gets those gooey puppy-dog eyes; the loneliness of knowing she has to keep the extent of her grief and anguish a secret, or else Mark will stop letting her visit, out of simple kindness.

What is it that keeps this sickness alive in her, she wonders? She's like one of those old songs that no one believes in.

Holly is jealous of Brenna, bitterly jealous, but she does not hate Brenna. Most of the time. Holly admires Brenna, in a way she shares Mark's love of Brenna. With Brenna, Holly reluctantly bows in submission to the worthier party. Looks may be subjective; brains may not be everything in matters of the heart. But Holly understands that, in some indefinable but unarguable way, Brenna is *better* than she is. She's the fuller-souled person, and that's all there is to it.

So Holly can accept that Mark prefers Brenna to herself. She can live with the perennial disappointment of having her fantasy voyages interrupted by the presence of Mark's actual lover.

It's something else to have to put up with this whining spoiled mute lunatic, who's ten or fifteen years younger than Holly and who can't bear to stop clinging to Mark in worshipful adoration, ever since he unfortunately rescued her. Holly can foresee that she will have no heart-to-hearts with Mark on this trip—the waif will shove her way into every exchange, she will worm herself into every crevice of this week in Long Beach.

Except that right now, she's nowhere to be seen. "Hello?" says Holly again, and remembers guiltily how she promised

Mark she'd look after the girl. What kind of face will Mark make if he discovers the helpless waif wandered off alone, because Holly was too busy sunbathing to keep her promise? She picks her way through the house into the living room.

And finds her there. Curled up on the sofa, legs pulled in to her belly. Face agonized; her mouth is moving, silently; with shock, Holly realizes that the only reason she is not whimpering and groaning is that she is mute. Even for that, she has no voice.

"Shit," says Holly, and squats before the girl, putting her face before the girl's to spare her the trouble of having to move her head. "Are you all right?"

The waif just looks at her with those doleful, pleading eyes. Earlier, she was scowling at Holly whenever Mark turned his back. At times Holly expected her to hiss. Holly tried to take Mark aside and explain it to him, convince him the girl was even weirder than he thought, but he assumed she was exaggerating. Besides, it was hard to take him aside, with that girl always hovering.

Now that the waif's in pain, though, with nobody but Holly here to help, there's none of that ferocious glaring. Only a mute, humble plea.

"Do you need me to call a doctor?" The waif looks at her like she's spoken Chinese. "Can you, like, make some signs, to show me where it hurts?"

The waif rubs her hands over her belly, craning her pathetic face towards Holly like a dying baby bird.

"Your stomach hurts? What was the last thing you ate?"

Instead of answering Holly in a way that makes sense, the waif nods her head furiously. She brings one of her hands to her mouth and mimes gobbling something.

Holly's confused. "So—you do think it's something you ate?"

A hurt, accusatory tinge comes into the waif's expression, as if she knows Holly must have gotten the message and she can't understand why Holly would nevertheless withhold her aid. She repeats the gobbling gesture, more pleadingly.

An idea comes to Holly. *No, it couldn't be. No way.* "*When* was the last time you ate?" she asks.

The waif stares at her, mournfully bewildered. More vigorously than ever she mimes gobbling something down, taking both hands and shoving an invisible mass of air into her chomping mouth.

Feeling stupid for even asking such a dumb question, Holly says, "Are you ... I mean, you're not just *hungry*, are you?"

The waif nods so enthusiastically she's bound to give herself a headache. Grabs Holly's wrist—her grip's surprisingly hard, it hurts.

"Really?!" Holly can't quite believe that. It's too weird even to be annoying. Who could be so helpless as to starve in a house with a fully-stocked kitchen and pantry? "Why didn't you eat that cheese sandwich Mark tried to give you then?" Who could hate cheese that much? Could she have some terrible allergy to dairy?

The waif only stares at her, despite a flicker of interest at the word "Mark." Holly gets the impression that the waif is desperately wondering why Holly isn't already feeding her, now that she's figured out what the problem is.

"Well, all right. Jesus, fine. Let's go to the kitchen. Can you walk?" Holly gestures at the waif to follow her, then waits to see if she can manage it. She can. She forces herself upright, bent over to hold her belly and still wobbly on her legs. Really, Holly ought to bring the girl some food. She might really be sick—Holly ought to call the doctor.

They get to the kitchen. The waif is still staring around like she doesn't know what they're doing here. The veneer of politeness that comes with the fact of Holly being a civilized person is starting to crack. "I mean, you are *hungry*, right?" she says.

The waif nods, wagging her head desperately, pleadingly.

"Well, so here we are. In the kitchen. You do know what a kitchen is, don't you?"

The waif shakes her head. Innocently.

Man, get the fuck out of here. Holly stares at the waif. "Are you fucking with me?"

The waif stares back, as if totally at Holly's mercy and without any clue what she's talking about.

"God damn it." Holly opens the cupboard above the sink. Bursting with cans. "Look. Food."

The waif stares blankly at the cans. Looks back to Holly for some hint. Looks back at the cans, straining as if to make out some food that might be hidden among them.

"I mean, are you allergic to any of this stuff?" asks Holly. "You can't be allergic to all of it, you wouldn't have lived this long."

The waif gazes at her in surrender, mutely asking why she's being so cruel.

"You don't want to eat any of this?" asks Holly.

Now a bit of a scowl comes back to the waif's expression when she looks at Holly, as if her tormentor is on the verge of pushing the absurdity of the joke too far.

At last, Holly begins to waver. Is it possible that the waif really doesn't get it? Maybe she's from someplace strange— they haven't heard her speak yet; obviously she understands English, but maybe if she were to speak they would hear an exotic Eastern European accent; maybe she was brought here by human traffickers. But where could she be from where she wouldn't have heard of cans? And where could she be from, where they wouldn't be cosmopolitan enough for canned food, but they would have English classes? Maybe her brain is addled. Maybe it isn't that a poisonous sea creature stung her, maybe it's that kidnappers plied her with drugs.

Trying to speak more nicely, Holly says, "How about fish? You like fish?"

The waif's eyes light up with voracious ecstasy, she starts furiously wagging her head again.

Holly takes a can of tuna from the shelf. On the label is a cartoon of a fat blue smiling tuna. "Here. You want this?" She holds the can out to the waif. "You want to eat this?"

The waif looks at the can and back up at Holly. Her expression gives Holly a chill. It says that never will the waif forgive this final mockery. Silent tears spill down her cheeks.

"Jesus, it's food!" exclaims Holly. She points at the can. "*That* is *food*."

The waif stares back at the can, confusion and frustration mounting. She turns it over in her hands, lifts it to her nose and smells it.

Dude, she's fucking smelling the can, thinks Holly. When it looks like the waif is about to take a ginger nibble, Holly snatches it back. "*Inside*," she said. "The food is *inside the can*. The tuna is. See the picture?" She holds the can up to the waif's face, points to the picture of the happy fat blue fish. "See the picture of the fish?"

The waif scrunches her face angrily at the blue shape. And then, with a gasp, her brow smooths, her eyes widen. As if this is the very first picture she's ever seen. Trembling with wonder, her hands begin to rise back up to the little can.

But Holly pulls it back. "Enough!" she cries. "Enough." She puts her hand on her forehead and takes a moment to collect herself. Then says, "Look. I'm going to show you how a can opener works. Okay?"

Five

Mark comes home, hours earlier than expected. Holly is happy to see him, for the usual reasons but mainly because she's still rattled by the business with the waif and would prefer not to be alone in the house with her. When Mark's truck pulls up she's on the front porch smoking. She's been there a while. There are seven butts floating in her makeshift ashtray, a plastic cup from the kitchen half-full of water.

"How's Pearl?" asks Mark, before saying hello.

"'Pearl'? Is that supposed to be her name? She told it to you? I thought she couldn't talk."

Mark looks disoriented, as if he's waking up. "I don't know," he says, "I feel like she.... No, I guess she didn't tell me her name, exactly. I guess I just sort of felt like it could be Pearl."

Holly gapes at him. Maybe the waif—or, fine, Pearl—maybe Pearl really does have something contagious. "Yeah, well, that's quite a specific guess," she says. "Because it's such a super-common name."

Only rarely is Holly short or sarcastic with Mark. But he doesn't seem to notice as he keeps moving to the door. Holly makes him pause by saying, "She's sleeping. She wasn't feeling well earlier."

Mark looks like they're talking about his day-old firstborn. "What was wrong with her?"

"She was hungry."

"Oh. But I tried to feed her that sandwich yesterday. And this morning I tried to give her some breakfast. An orange, eggs, cereal, toast...."

"That's not the shit she's into. She's into fish. And shrimp."

"Okay. Thanks. Good to know."

"Presumably she'd prefer it fresh, but the canned stuff will do the trick. You're going to need to re-stock your friends' pantry before they come back from Europe."

"How much did she eat?"

"All of it."

"What?" Mark gazes into the middle distance, re-seeing in his mind's eye the stock of canned seafood in George's and Albert's cupboard. There had been a lot.

Holly says, "Swear to God, she ate every thing in the house that had ever swum. Quite the cutesy carnivore. Of course, before that she had nearly starved to death because no one had ever explained cans to her before. Also pictures. She didn't know how to look at pictures until I explained them to her, so at first she had trouble telling what was inside which can."

Mark looks at Holly. He doesn't like hearing her talk about Pearl that way, and his displeasure makes his heart move a little further from her. "What do you mean?"

Holly can feel that increased distance—it goads her, as does the spectacle of him bending over backwards for the little castaway. "I mean she didn't know how pictures work," she says. "She did not comprehend that the two-dimensional image on the label was the stylized representation of a three-dimensional object, meant to convey information about what was inside the fucking can. I had to explain that to her. There's something wrong with her, Mark, she needs to be seen by a doctor."

He doesn't answer her; gazes into space, processing what she's told him. Holly feels like he's only interested in her insofar as she can give him updates on the waif.

"Anyway, why are you home so early?" she asks.

"I called someone, asked him to come cover for me."

Holly doesn't bother to ask why. "I didn't know lifeguards could do that. Switch shifts. Cover for each other like waiters."

"I never tried it before," says Mark. "But it worked." He

says this without looking at her as he opens the front door and goes inside.

Holly knows that he's not being deliberately, pointedly dismissive of her, that his thoughts honestly are elsewhere, and that's why he's so absent. That only makes it worse.

Inside, Mark stands still in the strangely shadowed living room, listening to the rhythm of Pearl's sleeping breath. He can hear her, in the room, but he hasn't seen her yet.

Holly doesn't seem to know he rescued that little boy the other day. Good—Mark prefers that everyone forget about it. Partly because of his usual modesty. But also, there was something unsettling about the experience. Once he'd grabbed the boy, when he was pulling him back to shore, he grew momentarily confused and paused, turned back to face the open sea. There was a weird tic in his brain; it was almost but not quite as if he'd hallucinated a beautiful voice, calling him back.

Pearl. It really is weird that he's started calling her Pearl. He knows that, he does; he frowns as he tries to think where he could have picked up the name. Anyway, it can't possibly really be hers. It must have come from inside him.

He steps forward until he can see where she's curled up asleep on the sofa, moist child-like mouth halfway open. Rather than disturb her, he creeps to the kitchen to check how much seafood is left and how badly Holly was exaggerating.

She wasn't. The floor is littered with more than a dozen empty cans. Mark assumes that Holly, despite what she said, must have eaten some of them. (She didn't. She did open them all. She tried showing the waif how to operate the manual can opener, but the waif couldn't get the hang of it. Or, rather, she never tried—just kept identifying the cans with pictures of happy sea creatures on the labels, and shaking them urgently in Holly's face, before Holly had even managed to open the backlog that had already accumulated, long after the waif simply must have sated her hunger. Disgusted, Holly left the empty cans where the waif had flung them upon slurping out the food within, picking it out with her fingers—if she had to open all the fucking things, she figured, let it be someone else's job to clean them up.)

Mark doesn't mind cleaning them up. Not now, though; it'll make a racket and awaken Pearl. The girl, that is—he reminds himself that "Pearl" is a name he came up with on his own, for unknown subconscious reasons. It couldn't possibly have anything to do with the waif, in real life.

He counts the empty cans, quits bothering before the end. Picks through them to confirm they're all empty. He checks the garbage to make sure nobody just dumped the contents in there. Maybe outside? Pearl couldn't possibly have eaten all this, Holly must have helped. But if somebody ate even half this much, they'd get really sick. He wants to go double-check on Pearl.

Not Pearl. That's a made-up name, she hasn't told them her name yet. The girl, the guest, the stray, the waif.

He stands over her sleeping form. He's not sure why she makes him so uneasy. He feels such a great tenderness for her. He supposes that's natural, under the circumstances, considering how lost she seems. But he's saved people's lives before, without ever feeling this sort of responsibility for them.

Of course, she's very beautiful. With her youth, her full gentle mouth, her straw-colored silken hair, her wide astounded delighted eyes. Her lithe little body. But she's really, really not his type—Marks' never been attracted to girls it seems he would have to take care of, and besides she's way too young for him. Not to mention, there's Brenna.

He squats so that his eyes can be level with her sleeping face. Gazes at her.

As if she knows he's going to be there before her, she opens her eyes and beams at him, passing without hesitation from sleep to wakefulness. Raises her head a bit so that it's inclined like a puppy's.

"Hey," he says. "You all right?"

30

Her grinning mouth half-purses, as if she has to hold in a shout of joy at this proof of his interest. She nods.

"Holly says you were hungry?"

There's a slight cloud at the mention of Holly, but it's dissolved by his presence and the act of talking with him.

"But you didn't want the sandwich I gave you yesterday, or this morning's breakfast?"

Not even the pleasure of his presence can stop her involuntary spasm of disgust.

"Okay. Duly noted.... But you didn't eat *all* that food, did you?"

She nods yes and rubs her belly, licks her lips, voluptuous and proud.

"All that canned tuna? All that canned shrimp? There must be almost twenty empty cans. Do you feel sick?"

She tilts her head at him like he's a silly old thing and she can't figure him out. Shakes her head.

Mark believes her about eating all that food, even though she is clearly not sick. On her breath he can smell the pungent reek of the mashed-up tuna, but somehow it doesn't bother him.

They're sitting here gazing deeply into one another's eyes. He's aware that it's weird they're doing that. The waif is beaming soulfully and adoringly at him; he has no idea what his expression looks like. He's aware that they're gazing at each other like this, but only in a distant, cerebral way. It feels like there are too many other confusing aspects of all this to worry about the mere social proprieties.

He looks at her. Opens his mouth, closes it. His question is too embarrassing to actually ask. He'd be embarrassed to ask it. He's not going to. Except then he figures, what the hell. And says, uncertainly, carefully, "Is your ... is your name Pearl?"

He only thought she was beaming before. Her face blossoms, in love, gratitude, joy. Her eyes moisten and her neck cranes toward his face. Mark draws back a moment after he should have, and even though they don't touch each other he's rattled by his own delay. It isn't that he wanted to kiss her. It's

31

more like it almost didn't occur to him to avoid it, like he failed to remember there was any reason for him not to let her kiss him.

Mark sits back on his heels. Brenna is right, he knows—this is ridiculous. How long is the girl going to stay here? There's no goal they're working towards, it's just this open-ended thing, she could be here till George and Albert get back, the way things are going. And then what?... Rationally, he knows that Brenna's right.

He studies Pearl. Notices how she drinks in his gaze, gets embarrassed. "So," he says. "You can't speak?"

She nods, enthusiastically, as if her muteness is a neat trick she's learned to do.

"Is it, like, a medical condition?"

She considers, then finally nods. As if that's not how she'd describe it, but it will do.

"Were you always unable to talk?"

She shakes her head, smiling fondly at him like that's a silly question.

"It's recent?"

She nods again, again as if it's a cause for celebration.

"Since less than a year?"

Nods.

"Less than a month?"

Nods.

"Less than a week?"

Nods.

Mark is incredulous. "Less than a week ago you could still talk?"

From her nod one would think her voice was a tumor she had barely managed to have cut out before it killed her.

"You just all of a sudden couldn't talk? Have you been to a doctor?"

Now she shakes her head as if he has passed the bounds even of silliness.

"Well, you have to go to a doctor."

She shakes her head.

"Listen, you can't be struck mute and then not even go to a doctor about it! I'm taking you to a doctor."

Not only does she shake her head, she grabs the sofa cushions, clenching handfuls of them in her hands as if to hold herself in place if he tries to carry her off. He can't tell if she's joking or not.

He rests his seat back on the floor and stares at her. He feels helpless, at a loss. There's this strange compulsion he feels to take care of her, yet she won't allow him to do the most elementary things.

Maybe the responsible thing would be to pick her up and forcibly carry her to a hospital, regardless of what she wants.... Yeah, right. As if he would drag her off someplace kicking and screaming, against her will.

Brenna is right. Naturally, as always, Brenna is right—sometimes that's comforting, sometimes it's maddening, but it's nearly always true. He should get on the phone and start calling doctors, hospitals, Human Services. He won't take her to the emergency room because there doesn't seem to be an emergency and because she doesn't want to go. It will likely be a long process so he should get started now. If he really has some big compulsion to take care of this stray, the only way to do that is to search till he finds someone who understands her condition. Clearly.

Before he can get on the phone, though, he gets lost in looking at her. Sitting there, gazing dreamily. She smiles, as if this is all natural.

It doesn't even occur to Mark to wonder how much time is passing.

The sound of the door snaps him out of his trance. He cranes over his shoulder to see Holly looking darkly at him and Pearl. She gets a soda from the kitchen fridge and goes back outside.

Mark turns back to Pearl and sees the last vestige of the disdainful expression with which she tracked Holly's movement. Now she beams at him again.

Mark gazes at her. There's something about her. And there's something about the way she acts like she's meant to be here, like washing up in front of the house Mark was house-sitting was some grand fulfillment of her destiny.

Experimentally, Mark says, "Pearl."

Again her visage is so swollen with joy it looks like it might kill her. She blinks tearful eyes.

Mark leans a few centimeters back away from her. It both moves and frightens him to be able to so easily provoke a reaction like that.

Obviously her name can't really be Pearl. She didn't, like, telepathically communicate it to him—he must have made it up, plucked it from his own subconscious. But if it makes her so happy, he supposes there's no reason not to call her that.

Without thinking, he says it again: "Pearl."

Six

When she wakes up, Brenna at first leaves the painting where it landed on the floor last night, avoids looking at it as she goes about her routine, acts as if it's invisible. Only after she's sat down and had her tea does she calmly go over, kneel on the paint-splattered floor, and look down at the canvas.

She's surprised to see how good it is. She assumed that her pride of the night before was at least partly due to the enthusiasm of creation, combined with whatever mental thing she was going through. But no, that blue maelstrom really is something. She doesn't even regret having painted over the female figure she was so proud of. There's something savage about it, wild, but powerful, almost regal.... "Regal"? What does that even mean? Fuck it, Brenna doesn't know, the word just came to her. She picks the painting up, goes and puts it back on the easel, stands back and regards it.

Now, as she looks at it, she feels herself becoming distant from herself, from both her body and her mind. As it did last night, the maelstrom again seems to move.

She jumps, shakes herself, twirls around and puts her back to the canvas. Laughs nervously at her own fear. But she is still scared. She's not sure what of, but she's not going to pretend she isn't.

Mid-afternoon, Brenna is on the road all the way back to Long Beach. That was always the plan, that she would head back up there after yoga, spend the night, spend most of the next day. But it was supposed to be a relaxing day at the beach. Even after Mark invited Holly, that's still what Brenna was expecting, irritated though she'd been—she'd been fantasizing about making love with Mark and then the two of them washing off the sweat and funk in the ocean, but Holly's presence would axe that. But that wasn't so bad; she likes Holly fine even if she disapproves of the way Mark deals with her. Now, though, she is heading up there for a real chore, going to help look after the waif. She has to admit, she's a little resentful.

All day she was tired. When teaching her class, she couldn't even demonstrate a head-stand. The place she teaches is laid-back and chill, so it isn't like anyone was scandalized. But it's a sign of what a rough condition she's in.

Maybe everyone was so forgiving of her lapse because of the bruise-like paint stains that are still on her head. Brenna explained to anyone who asked that it was paint, explained in a tone that conveyed she didn't want to talk about how the paint got there. Even after hearing the explanation, some people seemed to believe she'd fallen downstairs or been beaten by her boyfriend.

She pulls up in front of George's and Albert's, parking on the curb since Mark's truck and Holly's hatchback take up the driveway. Holly's out on the front porch smoking. She's sun-burned. Brenna says hello.

"What happened to your head?" asks Holly.

"It's paint."

Holly makes an almost exasperated face, as if she should have expected yet one more bizarre thing from the day. She nods towards the front door. "They're sleeping," she says. The derision isn't hard to hear.

"What?" says Brenna.

"Go on. Go check it out."

Brenna looks away from Holly and at the doorknob. She looks at it for several seconds. For some reason she's reluctant to reach out and turn it—she really doesn't know why. She finally does go in, of course.

Inside, the strangely shrouded house seems even more somber than usual, as if dusk came early here. Brenna steps deeper into it. Holly was right—the waif is asleep, curled up on the sofa, and Mark has gone to sleep on his side on the floor before her. The waif's pale hand dangles from the sofa's edge, her graceful fingers not quite touching Mark.

Brenna feels a pang. It's still true, what she said yesterday—she does trust Mark, and regardless of this tableau she doesn't believe anything is going on. Who knows why Mark went to sleep in such proximity to the waif, but she's sure there's an innocent reason. Still, it's not a sight most girlfriends would like to see.

Brenna goes back outside to join Holly on the porch.

"Still dreaming?" asks Holly, lighting another smoke. From the looks of her makeshift ashtray, she's smoked a pack today. Plus there are a bunch of empty soda cans littering the porch.

It strikes Brenna that Holly may wind up being the more irritating aspect of this saga. Look at her: moping, bitter, jealous, aggrieved. It's Brenna's boyfriend the waif is in love with; she doesn't let it ruin *her* day.

"He gave her a name," says Holly.

Brenna has been facing forward, the same as Holly; one of the depressing details of the moment is that they're facing out onto the ugly mundane street, instead of sitting behind the house from whence they can hear the majestic crashing of the ignored surf. Brenna turns to Holly. "What?" she says, a little sharply.

"Or, sorry, he sort of felt like what her name simply must be. Like, via a psychic vibe."

"What are you talking about, Holly?"

"Pearl. Mark says he just got a feeling her name was Pearl. I guess he made it up, because he says she didn't tell it to him. But she was pretty happy to answer to it."

Pearl. Why not Britney, or Tiffany? Still, they have to call the waif something. She says so to Holly.

In reply Holly laughs, not a very mirthful laugh, and turns to Brenna, shaking her head. "You know, I just don't get you."

"What's not to get?"

"You do know there's a hot twenty-year-old chick on the make for your boyfriend, and that they're sleeping next to each other in the next room. You know that, right?"

"Lots of girls have the hots for Mark," says Brenna, impatiently. She doesn't notice till after the words are spoken that it's a cruel thing to say. Holly clenches in embarrassment, puffs again on her smoke. Brenna continues: "I trust him."

"Trust him, fine. But you think he would never mess around on you? No matter how hard some nubile beauty threw herself at him?"

"I don't know if he *never* would. I guess we'll see. It's always his choice, after all. I wouldn't want him bound to me by some magic love potion he could never escape."

"I would," says Holly. She laughs that bitter laugh again. "Sorry, Brenna. I like you fine, but if I ever got my hands on some mind-controlling love potion, I would totally use it on Mark and steal him away.... I guess that's the point, though, right? Is that it would take something like that to get him away from you. And even then, who knows."

After Holly's outburst they're both quiet for a full two minutes, very embarrassed.

Brenna starts to open her mouth, thinking she'll tell Holly she's sorry about something; not an apology, but a "sorry" as in "I'm sorry to hear your whole family died." But she can't think what she would say, so she stands instead.

"I'm going inside," she says.

Holly nods, eyes forward. Still embarrassed for having said all that.

Back in the darkening living room, Brenna stands over the slumbering Mark. The waif, too, is still asleep on the sofa. Brenna regards them a while. The waif's fingers are outstretched towards Mark, but he isn't reaching for her.

Brenna squats beside Mark. She wants to talk to him, but prefers not to wake the girl. His mouth is open just a bit, like a new bloom. Gravity pools the flesh of his lips down into the lower corner. Brenna slips her index finger into his mouth, keeping on the safe side of his teeth, and lightly fishhooks him while tickling the cheek lining. He starts awake without making noise. She smiles at him. He smiles back.

Brenna has a funny feeling and looks up, then nearly jumps back. The waif is all of a sudden awake, too, and has silently risen onto her elbow and is glaring at Brenna.

No. Not the waif. Pearl. Without any idea how she knows it, without any reason to believe her own conviction, Brenna understands that Mark is right about that name.

After her initial fright, it pisses her off to be glared at that way. "Good morning," she snaps.

"Pearl," says Mark; then he seems to realize in what position Brenna has just found him. Still groggy, he looks around, confused. "I don't remember falling asleep," he says. He looks at the waif. "Did I fall asleep while I was talking to you?"

As if she's going to answer. She holds her angry eyes on Brenna an instant longer. Then she turns to once more beam at Mark.

Only now does Brenna start to feel the sort of reaction Holly probably thinks she ought to have. Not jealousy, exactly—as of yet, she has zero fear that Mark would ever cheat on her with this kid, although she's sure he wouldn't be angelic enough to avoid getting a hard-on, and getting his head turned by all the over-the-top adoration. No, what bothers her is not the chance of a rival, but the disrespect. The waif—fuck calling her Pearl, she's the waif—the waif alternates between acting like Brenna isn't there to see the moon-eyes being made at her boyfriend, and acting like Brenna murdered the waif's husband and now has the gall to show up at his funeral.

"Can I talk to you alone?" she says to Mark.

"Yeah, of course," says Mark. Then, startled and alarmed, he notices the stains. "What happened to your head?"

"It's paint."

"Okay," he says, getting to his feet. To the waif, he says, "Pearl, we'll be back."

It's gratifying to see how surprised and affronted she is that Mark would choose to go with Brenna instead of staying with her. But then Brenna notes an element of real pain in her expression and, though that exacerbates her annoyance even more, she can't exactly delight in it.

Mark seems discombobulated. It hurts Brenna's feelings that he should find the girl so flustering. It doesn't occur to her that her own discombobulation largely stems from the waif's presence, as well.

Outside, it's still a nice day. After being in that living room for five minutes, Brenna is half-surprised to find it's not yet dusk. They go out the back way, to go walk on the beach, and incidentally to avoid Holly, sulking on the front porch.

Mark isn't walking very fast, and he's almost even swaying. Brenna forgets about being miffed at him and starts to be genuinely concerned. "Are you all right?" she says, putting her hand on his back.

"Yeah, sure," he says. "I just, I don't know. I can't seem to wake up. That nap really did me in, I must have been *out*."

"How come you were sleeping so hard? Did you do something tiring today?"

"No. In fact, I didn't even finish the full day of work, I came home early because ... I don't know, I was worried."

That's a notable tidbit, but Brenna files it away for later. Right now, she's more interested in Mark crashing into sleep for no good reason. Though she knows she's being paranoid, she can't help but imagine some connection between the weird mental state that suggests, and her trance of the night before.

"Did you dream?" she asks. Casually.

Mark shakes his head. "No. Good old plain oblivion." Then his face changes. He's looking into some invisible distance. "Actually ... I think maybe I did have a dream."

Brenna waits, holding still. At last she says, "What about?"

Mark is still gazing off, trying to see something that is almost gone, or maybe only very well hidden. Slowly he says, "I think it was the sea...."

Brenna's breath fills her lungs like a cloud of tiny razors. Some disease, some virus, that gave both her and Mark the same dream? How could that be? In the brain, perhaps, a special clump of cells in which were centered all images of the sea, mother of life; a bacteria, a virus, which perverted that clump. An exotic sea-bred virus brought to them by Mark's latest dirty stray.

That's insane, of course. There must be something else going on. Something merely psychological.

"What about the sea?" she asks.

"I can't remember," he says, his face a puzzled scowl. They ought to be talking about this crazy situation, about what they're going to do about the waif. Instead they're here trying to tease out Mark's memory of his dream.

"Was it like you were going into the sea?" asks Brenna, even though she knows she shouldn't feed him images, she risks tainting the delicate, recalcitrant memories. But she can't help it.

"Um. Maybe," Mark says. Then he says, "No. It was like something was, like, talking to me from the sea. Except we were on land."

Brenna waits to see if he'll say more.

"I can't remember," Mark says, shaking his head, as if it matters, is something to be regretted.

Okay, that doesn't sound much like Brenna's dream. She's relieved but simultaneously almost disappointed—it would have been such a strange mystery if they'd had the same dream. But it isn't so odd that she and Mark should both dream of the ocean when Mark is a lifeguard spending a couple of weeks in a beach house.

Down to business. "You figured out the girl's name?" asks Brenna.

Mark looks sheepish. It's not a typical expression for him. "I don't know why, but I just started thinking of her as 'Pearl.' Obviously I must have made it up, but she seems more than happy to be called that."

41

"'Pearl.' You gave her a pretty name."

"Brenna's a pretty name, too."

Brenna looks at the surf. It looks more agitated than yesterday. She'd be reluctant to go swimming in it tonight. "So what are we going to do about her? About Pearl?"

"Keep on like we have been, I guess."

"Mark. What do you mean, exactly? You can't just mean letting her sleep over indefinitely."

"Why not?"

Brenna isn't looking at him at all anymore, only the ocean. She takes a couple of absent half-steps in the direction of the water. "What's going on, Mark?"

"Why do you ask me that? It's as big a mystery to me as it is to you. I don't know where she came from. I don't know why she can't speak. I don't know why it came over me to call her Pearl."

"You know that's not what I mean." Finally she looks at him again, and with a flash of anger and shock realizes that, no, he doesn't. "I mean what's going on with *you*, Mark?"

Is that a frightened look he gives her? "What?"

"What's going on with you and that girl?"

She didn't mean to use such a clichéd phrase, didn't intend the mundane accusation it implies. Just as she's beginning to be embarrassed, she can't help but notice the almost guilty look on Mark's face. Truly, she's never seen him like this before. It saddens her, and makes her feel angry that he's sullying the feelings she has for him.

"What do you mean?" he asks.

"I don't mean that I think you're cheating on me. But this girl clearly has some special meaning for you. Some meaning that isn't obvious."

"I just think she needs help, is all."

"And yet you refuse to get help for her. Even if she's not officially a missing person, there must be someone out there looking for her. There must be some reason she wandered into the ocean and then nearly drowned. She must have wandered in nearby—maybe she's been staying in one of these houses nearby, maybe she lives around here. There's clearly something off about her—she must have a condition that can be diagnosed. You don't seem interested in any of that stuff." She pauses, before pursuing her other question: "How did it come to you to give her a name, Mark?"

"I told you, it came to me."

"You were wondering what to call her and you picked the name Pearl? You just picked it for no reason?"

"That's not what I said. It came to me. I just, I don't know. I was sitting on the lifeguard chair, watching the swimmers, and all of a sudden I saw her face and heard the name 'Pearl.' The two things filled my head. After that I couldn't concentrate, just couldn't. It felt like I was supposed to be back here. So I called Peter on my cell, to come take over for me. And I headed back here."

There's a lull. Brenna watches Mark watch the waves.

Mark says, "Are you suspicious of me?"

"I'm confused."

"Do you think I'm hiding something?"

She hesitates. "Like I said, I don't think you're sleeping with her. Or plotting to. It isn't that." But if she doesn't think he's exactly hiding something, she does realize that something is hidden in him. Compulsions, needs to which she's never been privy, which she was never able to quicken in him but which the waif apparently does, which come so close to unmanning him that for the first time there are moments when he makes her want to avert her eyes, which makes her feel both guilty and betrayed. If he had consciously decided to fuck this girl, instead of being passively and helplessly fascinated by her, Brenna would be able to blame him and get angry instead of being merely sad and worried, and that's about the only difference. So maybe it would be better if he were fucking her.

She takes a step towards him. "I'm concerned about *you*, Mark. That's the thing I'm trying to tell you. I'm not particularly interested in that girl."

Mark sighs and nods, but as if to say that, while everything she says is true, there are aspects to this situation that she doesn't understand, that he can't explain. "I just feel responsible for her," he says, helplessly.

"But you're not."

"I know that, but I can't help feeling like I am. Anyway, we can talk about all this again in the morning. You're staying tonight, aren't you?"

"That's the plan." She's begun to feel less than thrilled about it.

"Actually," says Mark, "I was going to ask you ... maybe you could stay a little more than just tonight? Maybe you could stick around till we get the situation with Pearl sorted?"

It's all Brenna can do not to explode. He keeps badgering her about the same shit! "This sounds like an echo of a conversation we already had. And besides, I just finished *yet again* making clear my ideas of how we should sort out the situation with Pearl, and you vetoed those in favor of doing, uh, nothing. So remind me again what it is I'm supposed to be waiting around for?"

"Brenna. I know it's a lot to ask. But I'm telling you that I feel like I need you even though I can't explain why. Can't you accept that, this once? Can't we just consider this the worse in the 'for better or worse' part?"

"We're not married."

"All right."

"Can't you give me any specific hint at all of why you need me around? Originally I signed up for a romantic getaway. Then you invited Holly along—okay, I can deal with that, I like Holly fine. But this? This is crazy."

He can't seem to look her in the eyes. That, too, is unlike the Mark she knows. Speaking as if there's something blocking his throat, he says, "I'm just worried. About myself, what I might do. I'm worried about myself, around her."

Neither says anything else for a moment. The roar of the waves seems to grow nearer, paradoxically making their pause seem even more silent.

Brenna says, "Are you saying.... It sounds like you're saying you feel an overwhelming attraction to this girl, and you're afraid you won't be able to help giving in to it unless I'm here to police you."

Mark still won't look at her. "That's not exactly it," he says, with a mournfulness that makes her want to throw up.

"Wow," she says. "Wow."

"Brenna, please...."

"Frankly, it's not my concern who you fuck. I'm your girlfriend, not your probation officer."

"That's not...."

"I don't mean that I wouldn't care if you fucked someone else. I only mean it's not my concern. There's a difference. There's a difference."

Now she's the one who won't look at him. He says, softly, "I don't want to fuck anyone else, Brenna."

Conversation over, as far as she's concerned. Turns away from him to walk back to the house. Stops short as she realizes that going into the house means hanging out with the waif. Faces the sea again, says, "Would you mind going into the house? I feel like being alone."

"Come on, Brenna...."

"Please leave me alone. Go into the house. Talk to Pearl. At least she's not likely to say anything you don't like."

Mark half-turns to the house, heavy with the awareness of how badly he's fucked this up. She can still feel his eyes on her.

"Go, please," she says.

"All right. We'll talk about this later?"

"I don't imagine this is the last time we'll ever speak to each other, so, yes, we probably will."

Still he hesitates. But there's nothing he can say at this moment that will help. Slowly he trudges back up to the house.

Brenna stares at the ocean. Between the hypnotic surf and the strong emotions, time has started to work funny and she has no clear idea of its passage. At a certain point she becomes aware that the blue of the sky has gotten a little bit darker, the color of the sea more somber. Maybe movement will help whatever state she's in, so she forces herself to start taking steps to the water, turning this problem over in her mind.

It isn't the fact that Mark would be attracted to another woman that upsets her. Even if he were to give in to temptation and sleep with someone, it would hurt and infuriate her, but it wouldn't be the end of the world. And as for him telling her about it, well, she supposes she prefers honesty to dishonesty, given the choice.

What galls her is his helplessness about the whole thing. He comes to her like a little boy, not grown-up enough to be too embarrassed to ask his mommy to help him keep his penis in his pants.

She's walked almost to the edge of the waves' reach, the line where the wet sand meets the dry. She sits, not caring that she'll get sand in her clothes. The sea always has such a calming effect. She watches it swell and recede, inexorable, untroubled.

Maybe the sky is darker. Or it's a trick of her brain. How much time has passed? Who knows?

She looks at the sea, past the surf and out to the still line of the horizon. The waves are rhythmic, the line is calm. The combination soothes her mind. The problems seem distant.

Though she is looking straight out at the level sea from the shore, suddenly it is as if she is looking at it from above. She is dimly aware of the impossibility of seeing it from this vantage, but not particularly concerned by it.

In its center the flat wall of the sea begins to turn, a slow and stately maelstrom.

The center of the maelstrom dimples, drops, recedes out of sight. The maelstrom is a sort of tunnel in the water into the depths of the sea. Its watery walls turning, like a tubular funhouse corridor.

She dawdles at the entrance, unsure whether she's allowed inside. But then a voice comes: *Come, child.*

Still she hesitates for some reason.

Come in, the voice comes again. *Aren't you a good little girl?*

Then come in. For I have lost my own dear little girl, and need a new one to replace her.

But she isn't a little girl, Brenna protests.

But of course you are, says the voice. *You are to me. To me, you're all little. You'll always be little.*

And the voice is right, of course; he's right, she's always been a little girl. Content, she puts her thumb in her mouth and scratches herself absently.

She can't see whatever the voice is coming from (that doesn't bother her, she doesn't need to see), but clearly it's male. The voice is deep, paternal, confident, old, strong. Calming.

It is still speaking to her: *I need a new little girl. You are a good little girl, are you not?*

She nods her head, the exaggerated bobbing of a child.

Then come forth.

She can see him now, sort of. At least, she can make out hints of him. Something alive but born of rock, that doesn't like to move and does so slowly. Lit by light issuing from someplace other than the sun. Perhaps there isn't really any light at all, perhaps all light is banished from his presence, and what she "sees" is merely what pieces of the vision of him her mind has been granted. His stone is jumbled yet elegant. Odd life thrives in the temporary fiefdoms of his niches and crannies. Brenna tries to make sense of the whole of him but can't, his geometry doesn't fit right. Perhaps because she is so tired, so distracted. What is it that's distracting her?

Why do you not come forth?

He does not sound displeased yet, only amused and curious. Brenna would not want something so worthy to feel displeased with her. One thumb still in her mouth, she attempts a curtsy. Then begins to girlishly waddle forth.

That's it. Good, obedient child. Nothing shall ever replace that other little girl. But having you here will be a comfort to me.

A rhythmic roaring grows louder in her ears, grows less rhythmic and more into a steady unstopping blare. And yet she can still hear that stone's voice as clearly as ever, as if it could never be muffled by mere noise.

Obedient child. Now, that other—she never was that. You have her quite trounced in that regard. A beautiful girl. But headstrong.

Brenna is still moving forward, but she seems to be sinking as well. Her legs continue to move, but they seem to have less and less to do with the motion of her body. That roaring fills her mouth, and there is some dark pressure being applied to some part of her mind, not unpleasantly. That pressure keeps her calm.

Headstrong. And spoiled. For I have never been able to refuse her anything she asks.

A wisp of sound, a microscopic razor sneaking in and tearing the black curtain of her calm. Suddenly that pressure feels less comfortable, suddenly it seems localized in parts of her physical body. Maybe her face. Maybe her chest.

What are you listening to? Foolish girl, do you believe anything out there is real?

That sound comes again. She has a vision of a coach blowing a whistle. But no, she knows that voice. That's Holly.

Holly's screaming. Is Holly okay?

No sooner has she seen in her mind the picture of Holly screaming on the beach at George's and Albert's house, the house where Mark is, than she finds herself no longer in a child's body but her own, and that formerly gentle pressure turns itself into an onslaught of claws, amorphous and irresistibly strong, shoving and punching their way into her mouth, nose, lungs.

Her limbs spasm back to life. The tide surges her up, and as her head breaks the surface of the water the thick, distant sound of Holly's cry comes threading through the surf: "Mark! She's there! There!" How dark the sky has grown. Again the sea yanks her below.

A hand grabs her shirt, then hooks under her arm and around her chest. She is being dragged, someone is making sure her head stays above water. Her eyes sting with salt. When she can keep them open she leaves them on the dark sky. Dark purple, like a dark rich formal bruise.

She knows it's Mark, and that he's dragging her through the surf to shore. But she hasn't really come back to herself yet, and facts still don't have significance. It occurs to her that it's rude to make Mark do all the work, and she starts moving her arms and legs, trying to swim on her own. She's mildly surprised by how weak and uncoordinated she is, and her erratic movement probably does more to hinder Mark than to help him.

Soon he's dragging her onto the sand.

He stops while her legs are still being submerged and released, submerged and released by the tide. Mark's face fills her vision suddenly. He's scared but not panicked. Probably only she knows him well enough to be able to tell how scared he is, she reflects with pride. Most people would see only the cool, efficient way he goes about checking her pupils, her breathing.

Once he's completed his immediate exam his head recedes and he simply stares down at her, with bewildered concern. Above him Brenna sees Holly standing over her, hand on her mouth.

Everything shakes, she realizes everything has been periodically shaking, for some time. She's been coughing, coughing up seawater. Her throat is raw, red, tastes like the sea.

"What were you doing?" demands Mark.

She stops coughing. Makes her eyes focus on Mark. Repeats the question: "What was I doing?"

"You went swimming, with all your clothes on? You went swimming in your jeans? And then, what? You got caught in a current?"

Brenna listens to him. Without moving, she tries to take stock of her body. Yes, she can feel those wet heavy jeans, cooling and tightening on her legs. They've been dragged almost down below her hips, it's a wonder they're still on at all. The top of her ass-crack is exposed to the wet sand. Her

T-shirt has been soaked, twisted and has ridden up so high it's almost choking her, her bra and belly exposed to the sky.

"I … went swimming?" she says.

"Yes," says Mark. "I guess you did. That, or … what else would you have been doing?"

"She was just floating out there," says Holly, still freaked out. "Just letting those waves throw her around. If I hadn't happened to walk around back and just happened to see her, then.... Jesus, Brenna, were you even conscious?!"

Brenna feels like the world has been trickling back in, and now it's coming in a flood. Suddenly she's gasping and thrashing to get her legs out of the water.

Mark's trying to hold her still. "Brenna!" he says.

"Get me out of the water!" she shouts. "Get me out of the water!"

"All right!" Mark helps her get out of the reach of the waves.

Sitting on the dry sand, Mark kneeling beside her, Brenna starts to tremble. "Where is he?"

"Where is who?" asks Mark. When she doesn't answer, he repeats himself: "Where is who? Was somebody out here with you? Did someone take you out into the water?"

"I don't know." Brenna screws her face up, concentrating. "I'm trying to remember."

Mark waits, trying to be patient. But after a moment she only shakes her head and says, "I can't remember."

The sea fills her vision again. Again she recoils from it, though she regains enough control of herself not to scramble away. "I've got to get out of here."

"What?" says Mark.

"Home," she says. She's sure as shit not sleeping at the beach tonight.

"Brenna, I don't know. I'm worried about you, I don't know if you should...."

"I'm going," she says. Rises to her feet, brushes off Mark's hand when he tries to support her. Legs are shaky, but they'll do. "I'm out of here."

She turns and begins walking back towards the house, yanking her tangled shirt back down. At first Mark and Holly only watch her go. As Brenna gets closer to the house her eyes stray over to the porch and she nearly jumps. All of a sudden the fucking waif is out there, leaning on the rail, eyeing her with malicious amusement. Like the only thing that could have made her day better would have been if Brenna had *actually* drowned.

Instead of going around the house as she'd intended, Brenna marches up to the porch where the waif is standing. With cool disdain the waif watches her approach.

Once she's only a foot away from her, Brenna looks the waif in the eyes and says, "You're a fucking cunt." The waif's pale face flushes with anger. Brenna continues around the house to her car.

It's really dusk. How long has it been since she sat on the sand after her talk with Mark? She'd like to ask, but getting the fuck out takes precedence.

Mark's beside her now. "Brenna. Are you sure you can drive?"

"Sure am."

"I don't want to leave you alone after that."

"So get in the car with me."

They're at the car now. Brenna is digging in the pocket of her soggy jeans for the keys—the pocket lining is all twisted around and impossible to set right and smooth out because it's a wet wad. Thank God the keys didn't fall out into the ocean, the pants didn't come off. Everything in her wallet will be soaked, too. "Get in the car with me."

"I don't think I should leave."

"George and Albert will understand. I'll fucking explain it. Or try, anyway. If I can get someone to explain it to me, first."

"It's not that, it's...." He shrugs as he trails off.

Not being able to work the keys loose adds to the fury she's trying to keep reined in. "I know what it is," she snaps. "It's your little project in there."

"Come on, Brenna. It's a crazy situation, let's both be flexible...."

"*I almost fucking drowned*," she shouts. He looks stricken again. "But, hey, don't worry about that, stick around keep an eye on fucking Pearl. She really needs your presence because—uh, why was it again? Oh, never mind, I forgot—you can't quite put it in words."

"Hey, I know you almost drowned, because I'm the one who just rescued you."

Finally she gets the keys loose, tugging as violently as if she were having to rip them out from inside her body. "Brenna," says Mark, as she gets the door open, sits, and slams it again. Again he says her name as she turns the key in the ignition. She puts the car in reverse and backs out.

Her passenger-side window is open; as she's reversing onto the street, before she can take off, Mark reaches into the car to unlock the door. She slaps her hand across the car and over the lock. "Get your hand out of the car," she says.

"Brenna. Wait a second."

"No." Foot on the brake, she takes her hand off the wheel so she can switch gears into drive without releasing the lock. Putting her hand back on the steering wheel, she lets the car drift forward, very slowly. "Let go of the car, Mark."

"Listen, I'll get in the car with you. Like you asked. I'll go with you."

"That offer expired." She has to go slow to avoid injuring Mark, but it's dangerous to drive like this anyway, with her arms spread across the breadth of the car, her face positioned close to the center of the windshield. She's not used to looking at the road from this angle, and it's hard to control the wheel with her arm extended this way. Luckily it's a quiet street with no traffic at the moment. "Let the fuck go of the car, Mark."

"No. I'm worried. Take me with you. Let me in."

For a frightening instant she has the psychotic urge to slam on the accelerator and teach him a lesson. The image of what that might do to him, if she dragged him along the road or if his legs got under the wheels, pumps vomit up her throat that has to be swallowed back. "Fucking let go of my car, Mark! Fucking let go of it!"

He obeys. She makes herself wait till she's sure he's free of the car, then slams on the accelerator. She actually peels out, only the second or third time in her life she's ever done that.

In her rearview mirror she can see Mark, standing in the street, watching her go.

Seven

Brenna drives home. She curses the length of the drive; she feels that it's all she can do to keep concentrating enough to keep the car on the road, that if she gives her mind any free play it will slip out of her control and the car will plow into something. By the time she gets home to Coney Island she's exhausted.

It isn't like she can go to sleep, though. She does try to lie down on her cot, after she's peeled off her wet salty clothes and taken a shower. But her mind is an angry storm of the waif, Mark, the strange unremembered dream, waking up to find her throat and lungs being raped by the sea.

She turns the light back on and starts doing yoga exercises. It's getting late, and she's been tired all day anyway, so it seems like a work-out should knock her out nicely. Doesn't work, though. After a half-hour of exercise she decides to calm herself with meditation. Just fifteen minutes or so. She sits in her corner, closes her eyes. But as she nears the meditative state, it's as if she feels something tickling at her mind. She knows she ought to let it come, it's stupid to be scared of one's own mind. But whatever it is, it reminds her of what happened to her at the beach, when she woke up in the sea. She snaps her eyes open and stands up.

Sleep still is not an option, and she has to do something. She gets a blank canvas on the easel and preps her oils and brushes.

It's late to be starting on a painting. And if she suddenly crashes, it'll be a pain in the ass getting everything cleaned up so she can finally get to bed. But fuck it. She doesn't have any work tomorrow, she can sleep through the whole day if she likes. She had planned to spend it in Long Beach, but now she's free.

She sets up with no idea what she wants to paint. Just doodle till she gets sleepy.

Looks at the palette. The blue gives her a chill. That's silly. Still, she mixes a reddish-pink instead. That's the least sea-related color she can think of (though that's a foolish though, for all colors are of the sea). Now she realizes that she's been avoiding the sight of her canvas from the night before, that her eyes have avoided sweeping that corner of the apartment even though the canvas is facing the wall. She doesn't look now, either.

With her brush she makes a line on the canvas. She's left the paint incompletely mixed, so there are strings of red in it, like blood. Keeping only loose mental control of her hand, she lets it trace a dancing sinuous line. It reminds her of a tentacle. She lets the line grow through the whole canvas.

A noise like the inside of a conch has been growing in her ear. For some reason, she's not concerned that her hearing is wonky. The roar builds. Her hand slows. The blood-streaked tentacle moves with her hand along the canvas and then, as Brenna's hand floats off the surface, it continues invisibly into the room.

Brenna stands still, muscles loose, eyes glazed, not seeing anything in the apartment.

Very very high above, sunlight enters the world like broken jewels.

A voice whispers: *Whenever I can....*

A sudden tentacle flashes before Brenna's vision. Far away, in her apartment, her body gives a tiny gasp. Brenna nearly snaps back into it, like a rubber band broken by high tension.

But the sibilant soothing voice hushes her: *No, no, no fear ... no fear ... I would not harm you.... Now be still, for it is difficult for me to contact you. I can manage it only when* he *is preoccupied.*

Brenna is granted a vision of thousands of creatures passing in review before a king of stone and fossilized coral. With their powerful tails they shoot through water so pressurized that it's like passing through a wall; in their muscular arms they hold spears and prods with which they herd the prizes of the King, the wrathful tentacled behemoths. It is a parade devoted to the glory of the King, and it will last a long time.

The voice, a female voice, recommences its whispering: *Whenever I can, I listen to the singing of those many daughters. It is forbidden for one such as I to come too near them, but I have my ways and I take my risks. For the singing of such daughters is worthy of risk. Many are the human sailors who have run their boats upon reefs and rocks, that they might hear those songs—and those are creatures of such a paltry span. For those such as I, for whom the millennia pile up and up, risks become ever more necessary.*

So when one such daughter steals away from her keepers and the court, and comes to seek me in the slimy places to ask a trade, the price I ask is always her voice.

Especially for this daughter, who had such an extravagant demand. To wear a form in which she might walk the sands and meet that mortal hero she'd seen flapping his land-born limbs through the very edges of our realm. Glimpsed him oh-so-heroically rescuing a human child from the gentle grip of her father.

She thought she drove a hard bargain, making me agree that if, at the end of a certain term, she had won her hero's heart, I would render her back her voice, and she would be free to bring him back to our world, if she chose.

But if, when the dusk of the fourth night neared, she had not yet made her conquest, I would keep her pretty voice forever. And her soul would evaporate into nothing as her pretty body dissolved into foam.

Ah, how perfect that would be! For, though I love the voices of those daughters, I hate all else about them. Especially this one.

So confident was she. How easy she thought it would be, to go into a strange world as an ignorant mute, and seduce that man. As if all she need do were present herself to any creature, and it would adore, worship, and fear her. She is a brat who has never understood that the honors paid to her are born only of the fear her worshippers feel of the father. I thought I was all but guaranteed to spend the rest of my eternity listening to that sweet song whenever I wish to open my treasure box; not only that, but to have the pleasure of watching her precious features become nothing but a slick upon the surface of the sea....

Frankly, my child, you're letting me down. I ran my fingers through your young man's heart before I made this deal, and saw the place you hold there. It was for that reason that I felt I had a safe bargain. I expected you would fight, when you saw the daughter trying to usurp your place. It would take so little effort, to rebuff her—you could stop her, even despite that power she inherited from her father, to cloud mortal minds and turn mortal gazes. But you seem unwilling to make that effort. Is it pride? Perhaps the fashions of ladies have changed since last I cast my eyes upon the land—for I confess that was a long, long time ago....

Do as you will, but heed my warning—if she wins his heart, the pact is sealed and he is hers forever. She will be allowed to bring him down to our realm, where you shall never see him again. She shall do as she pleases with him, for he shall be forever in her thrall.... And he shall not have a princely life here below, for her disobedience has banished her forever from her father's court, though the spoiled fool likely still believes the King will relent....

But if you can keep your ascendance for tonight, tomorrow night, and the following day, she shall trouble none of us, evermore.... Except once—for, though I say she shall never have that lovely voice again, when her time is up I'll give her one last cry that even her father will hear, in his depths....

Ah, the sentinels of the King have heard me—they shall stifle our talk.... But remember, child ... remember my words ... remember now, with prudence ... or later, with regret....

Gradually, patches of the room begin to melt back into Brenna's view: a piece of wall here, a lamp there. Whatever dark and fluctuating things she's been seeing in their places are already slipping from her mind.

Before her is the canvas with the pink red-streaked line. She takes a step backward, drops her palette and brush.

Moving briskly, she gets a notebook and pen and begins

writing down all she can remember of what the voice said. Those words are trying to fade as the ambiguous sights did, but she concentrates on holding them in place till she can get them down.

The fuck, she thinks. *What the fuck?* But she refuses to dwell on the craziness of what she's writing. Her focus now is on getting it down: later on she can show it to a shrink, or Mark, or a guru, or whoever.

She finishes. She reads over what she's written. When she gets to the passage about the King's preoccupation, she vaguely remembers the procession and then, suddenly, vividly, she flashes on a shadowy cephalopod as big as a skyscraper, and her belly clenches with fear.

The fuck. What the fuck.

She calls Mark. His voicemail picks up. At the beep, she says, "Hey. Listen. Call me back, I want to talk about what's going on." After a pause, she says, "I don't necessarily mean that I want to exchange apologies, or talk about how we personally feel about what's going on, or anything like that. I'm more interested in the practical question of what we're going to do about, uh, about Pearl. I'm starting to think this is something we can't just agree to disagree about."

Before hanging up, she considers saying "I love you," but doesn't. He knows she loves him; like she said, she doesn't want to distract either of them with a make-up session, she wants to get down to business and figure out how to get that waif out of the house. Once she's hung up, she regrets not having said it, but doesn't call back.

Now she's alone in her small apartment, bright with all the lamps. Trapped in here with her own mind. She glances up at the new canvas, then drops her eyes. Sitting cross-legged on the floor, she crosses her arms over her chest and slumps forward, rounding her back and letting her head hang.

"I'm scared," she says. Her voice is small, breath and vocal chords constricted by her posture. "I'm scared. But okay. Fuck it. I'm scared, but that's okay."

Admitting how frightened she is calms her somewhat. She stands, undresses for bed even though she's not sure she can sleep, so wired and adrenalized is she from her weird waking nightmare. "I'm scared," she says, as she turns off all the lights. Once the room is in total darkness, she has second thoughts and re-lights the smallest one as a night-light. "Because I'm scared," she explains matter-of-factly to the empty room.

She lies on her cot face-up with her eyes open, staring up at the dimly-lit ceiling. "I'm scared," she says calmly. "I'm scared." After a very long time she closes her eyes. "I'm scared." Every once in a while she'll just say it. "I'm scared." Gradually, she says it more softly, she enunciates less clearly: "I'm scared...." She keeps saying it every so often, until, eventually, she goes to sleep.

Eight

Holly watches Mark. She keeps an eye on him and the waif. It's no longer about jealousy, not mainly. Though she can't put a finger on why, she's worried about Mark, and doesn't think the waif is having a good effect on him.

There was that fight he had with Brenna. Holly has fantasized many, many times about Mark and Brenna breaking up. But now she finds that the specter of it actually occurring is different from the fantasy. Anyone can see that Mark and Brenna are in love, that they probably have been since they met, and that Brenna is the best thing ever to happen to Mark. A bitter truth, but there it is.

Besides, if Brenna and Mark do break up, it won't be like he's dumping Brenna so he can be with Holly.

At first, Holly avoided the waif because she made Holly uneasy. But now that she's realized her own presence sets the waif on edge, she finds it a bit less unpleasant to impose herself on the other guest.

It's sickening, the way the waif gazes at Mark, the way she constantly tries to touch him even though he usually recoils, or draws his hand back, or whatever. At times Mark looks so irritated, Holly thinks he's on the verge of telling the waif to fuck off. But then some invisible thing will happen, and he'll start gazing at her all mooney-eyed. For a few inexplicable moments he'll be almost as bad as her.

Holly has no idea how, but she's sure the waif is fucking with his head. Like, chemically, or with hypnosis, or something—something serious.

Like, he seems confused a lot of the time. Holly will try

to say something to him, and at first he won't even notice, as if he's got loud headphones on. Then he'll look at her, startled, and say, "What?" At first Holly was trying to get his attention once in a while as a somewhat petulant challenge. But now she's started doing it out of real concern, trying to recall him from wherever he's floated off to.

Sometimes Mark will pick up his phone, with what looks like resolve. Holly assumes it's to call Brenna. But he always gets distracted by something, by some unheard noise, and winds up checking on the waif instead.

One time, after going out of the room with his phone, he returns to the room too soon to have called anyone and, looking at Pearl, says, "Did you say something?" Holly gapes in amazement. The waif is fucking mute and hasn't made a peep. But Pearl smiles sweetly and shakes her head, as if it's the most natural question in the world.

Mark retreats to the beach behind the house. Pearl follows him outside. From the window Holly watches them. Mark keeps pointing at the house—muffled through the pane, Holly can make him out, asking the girl to go back inside and wait. She clings to him, silently begging him to let her walk along the beach with him. He removes her arms, gently, firmly, with a pained expression. Like a doting father heartbroken at having to deny his daughter something for the first time. Finally his frustrated exasperation grows strong enough that it frays through the gentleness of his tone; he points his arm ramrod-straight back to the house. Pearl trudges back, hanging her head pathetically, looking back over her shoulder every couple seconds. Mark shakes his head in exasperation, or to clear it, or both. Holly watches him stalk down in the direction of the water.

Pearl comes back inside and flings herself onto the sofa, pouting with her arms crossed tight across her chest. Noticing Holly looking at her, she scowls fiercely and throws herself onto her side and turns, so that she's reclining with her face towards the back cushion. Her shoulders shake. She's sobbing quietly.

Holly stares at her. What a helpless waste of skin. It's inconceivable that someone like Mark could be as hung up on that girl as he appears to be.

Looking out the window at him, it strikes her that it's inconceivable to him, too. He's out there pacing back and forth, articulating, talking to himself. It's weird to see someone manically pacing on a beach—you're supposed to be relaxed on a beach. Because Holly's in love with Mark, for lack of a better term, it doesn't hit her how crazy he looks. But it's plain that he's very upset.

After a minute of watching Mark, of taking in just how nuts Pearl is making him, Holly turns back to the waif with a sour curl on her lips. The girl's shoulders have stopped shaking—Holly assumes she's still sulking, but supposes she could be asleep.

"You know," she says, "I have a thing for Mark, too."

Pearl twists her head around to give Holly a brief, disdainful look. As if to say that of course Holly has a thing for Mark, but someone of her caliber isn't worth Pearl's worry. She turns back to face the cushion again and scrunches further into the sofa.

Holly smiles. *You gotta hand it to the kid*, she thinks sarcastically, *she's not afraid to show a little attitude*. She says, "I even got to sleep with him one time."

Pearl turns to glare at her more quickly this time.

Holly holds her gaze and laughs. "That got your attention, huh?"

Holly looks away from Pearl. She can still feel the waif's glare on her as she picks at the fringe of one of George's and Albert's throw pillows. "Yup. That was about five damn years ago now. Jesus—five years. Feels like last night, you know?

"He was my yoga instructor, he'd been my yoga instructor for like three months, and I guess I had a little crush on him. I mean, you of all people can understand that—right? After class I would always find excuses to chat with him, I'd ask him if he wanted to grab a coffee—he'd always be like, Nah, can't really today, got a client, gotta run. I figured he either thought it might be awkward, what with me being a pupil, or else he just wasn't that into me. I kept plugging away, though. Total shameless hussy.

"Finally I had a show I was stage-managing, and I gave him a flyer for it and talked it up—it was just some shitty little Off-Off-Broadway thing out in Queens. And, you know, he's such a nice guy, he actually came to it. After the show I raced out of the tech booth to talk to him—I mean, I raced out in a casual, suave way. He said he'd thought I was actually *in* the show. He was kind of laughing when he said it, he knew what I'd been up to. I told him that, while I hadn't actually technically fibbed, I had maybe kinda-sorta made it sound like I was actually performing in order to increase the chances he'd show up. And that to make up for my harmless little deception I was forcing him to let me buy him dinner. 'Resistance is futile,' I told him."

Holly trails off. Sort of caressing the throw pillow. She can still feel Pearl's eyes on her, but isn't paying much attention. Although she started telling her tale merely so as to gall the waif, now she's gotten lost in it again.

Voice further away, she says, "Even when I took him home, I could tell he was kind of doing it to be nice. Not that I'm ugly or anything, just more like he could take it or leave it. And maybe it's pathetic, but that didn't turn me off at all. Not at all. I liked that he wasn't a horn-dog. And I also liked it that he, you know, that he was kind."

Again she stops talking. Starts to turn again to gaze out the window at Mark, but stops herself.

She says, "However good you're thinking it would be—it was better. A bunch of daydreams sprouted that night and over the next couple days, while I was looking forward to seeing him again. And can you believe it? During those couple days he met Brenna for the first time. Just being casually introduced to her at a party was all it took to bump me out of the running for good. That was totally obvious from the start. Even so, it was hard for me to accept it—so I do understand at least that one particular aspect of your little fixation. I'm not much better, in terms of unrealisticness. Like, I almost turned down my good job in Philly because it meant giving up the disgustingly Platonic coffees me and him used to have every three weeks."

Holly levels her gaze at Pearl. "You want to know why Brenna never minded me getting those coffees with her boyfriend? Even though I'm a smart, passably hot girl who's as open as you can politely be about the fact that I would happily fuck him, even if it was only just the once and I could never tell anyone? You know why it didn't bug her that I was going to be staying here alone with him? It's because she knows how totally in love with her he is. And that she has nothing to worry about.

"It's actually kind of a beautiful thing. Like, if I were capable of some objective viewpoint, I'd probably feel happy. Because it all worked out so obviously for the best."

Pearl is seething. She may have no voice, but Holly can hear her breath from across the room.

Holly smiles evilly at her. She doesn't mind a fight.

"But with you," she said, "I have no trouble achieving an objective viewpoint, and being happy that you will never, ever bag him. Because you won't. So why don't you quit bothering him? Whatever terrible thing you're managing to do to him, why don't you stop? If you really gave a shit about him, you would."

Pearl's glare has grown so intense that it's scary. Rather than letting that give her pause, Holly rides the wave of the murderous fury emanating from her little friend.

She leans in Pearl's direction. "You're not going to fuck up Mark and Brenna," she says. "You'll do that over my dead body."

Pearl glares even harder than ever. Holly wonders if she's gone too far. Pearl is breathing in and out so fast and hard that she sounds like a very small bellows. Something funny is happening with her eyes. It looks simultaneously like they're caving in and like they're popping out. That doesn't make any sense, though, and Holly can't quite pinpoint or articulate what she's seeing, so she must be making it up.

Determined not to reveal her uneasiness, Holly forces herself to maintain eye contact with Pearl as she gets up. Gets up and goes to the front door and outside. Out to the front porch, where she can breathe a sigh of relief at getting away from the creepy waif, but without disturbing Mark's pacing.

Nine

Brenna sleeps fitfully—in fact, she barely sleeps at all, so often does she keep jumping and flinching, without quite waking up. Whatever the bad dreams are, she can never remember them. Several times during the night she's compelled to get up and make sure the door's locked, because in her sleep she thought she heard knocking. Half-awake, she yelps at a monstrous shadow cast by the night-light, and considers turning it off. But without the light it would be worse.

She becomes aware of daylight seeping into the apartment, and isn't sure if it's waking her up or if she's been awake for a long time already. Dazed with exhaustion—not only from lack of sleep, but from the night's inexplicable terrors—she lowers herself off the cot, first a knee onto the floor, then a hand, then the other hand, other knee; then she curls up on the cold linoleum. It's a trick she has, when she doesn't want to get up yet—if she lays on that cold floor she'll want to rouse herself soon enough.

But this morning she remains there far longer than she normally would, staring ahead. Trying to think of what she should do when she gets up. She has no particular plan for today, not anymore. The plan had been for her to wake up beside Mark in Long Beach and spend the day at the beach.

Finally, she forces herself to sit up. It's nonsense, freezing to death on the floor that way. She knows perfectly well what she ought to do. She'll go take an extra yoga class—she'll sit in the park—she'll catch up on her reading. Maybe she'll go see a movie. At some point she'll call Mark, to prevent their spat—well, fight—from swelling to epic proportions. But, after checking the state of her feelings, her levels of anger and woundedness, she decides that the call should wait till later in the day.

She knows there's a yoga class at noon. She grabs her rolled-up mat and throws her book in her tote bag. She picks up her phone and looks at it for a long, hesitant moment. Sometimes she leaves her phone behind her, at the apartment. It relaxes her, not being driven to look at it every five minutes. Maybe that's what she needs today. On the other hand, maybe all the stuff going on with the waif, along with the fight she and Mark had, means that she should keep the phone with her. Just in case.

But no. If she talks to Mark in the next few hours she'll just yell at him. Probably she should give things some time to settle. If she has the phone with her she won't be able to resist the temptation to call before she's calmed down a bit.

As for the possibility of there being some problem with the waif, the waif isn't her responsibility. Besides, as she's told Mark multiple times, whatever the waif's problems may be, Brenna isn't qualified to deal with them.

So she turns her phone off and leaves it on the card table in her kitchen area. Before leaving, she gives it a last look. Something tells her leaving it there isn't such a good idea. She starts to go back for it. But then it's like something else stops her. She tells herself that it's simply her own resolve, to follow through on her own decision, and steps out into the hall and locks the front door behind her, without the phone.

During the train ride to Union Square she has a hard time keeping attention on her book, an essay on meditative practices. Once the long ride's over and she's sitting in the park, she hopes the beautiful weather and bustling people will snap her out of her funk, but she still can't focus on the words in her book and feels increasingly gnawed by worry. Yoga will help, she tells herself, and is relieved when it's finally close enough to noon for her to go to the studio. But the hour-and-a-half session is hell. The anxiety mounts and mounts, it's as if all the blood in her body has been replaced by a grating yellow energy pulsing through her, vague and awful premonitions waxing and waning inside.

The worst is the end, when the teacher tries to lead them through a brief meditation to finish. As Brenna begins to clear her mind, she can feel some invasive thing ready to prod its way in. Now it seems to her that it's been lying in wait the whole time, waiting to pounce upon her as her vinyasa practice softened her attention—that's why this class has been so exhausting and difficult. She jumps up from her mat and hurries out of the room, her teacher and classmates watching her with concerned surprise.

She wishes she hadn't left the phone. She doesn't even know Mark's fucking phone number, she probably hasn't looked at it once since she saved it, five years ago. Imagine, not knowing her own boyfriend's phone number!

She hurries through the subway station. The tension mounts every time the train lurches to a halt at a stop that isn't hers. Who knows what development someone might have called to tell her about.

For whatever reason, she just has a feeling something serious is going on.

It's all a little humbling. Without meaning to, she tends to look with a gentle disdain at the hordes of people hunched over their smartphones. Now here she is, worse than any of them.

Arriving at her apartment, she moves briskly to the table with the phone. There are eight missed calls. On the one hand her heart sinks to see so many—surely it means something is wrong. On the other hand, after being torn up with curiosity, it gratifies her to see that she's about to find out what is happening.

But those calls leave her still more bewildered and uneasy.

Holly has called five times, without leaving a message. She wouldn't have called so many times if there'd been nothing going on. Brenna tries to comfort herself with the reasoning that, if there were something truly serious, she would have left a voicemail.

But maybe it was something she couldn't explain. Or maybe something hurtful, that she couldn't bring herself to say.

Mark has called three times. The first two times he hung up when the voicemail answered—he must have really wanted her to pick up. The third time he finally gave in and left a message. It's a strange one.

It's a little hard to hear. In the background is a hissing roar, steadily swelling and falling. It's the surf, Brenna realizes; he's called from outside, from the beach. She has a funny, paranoid idea that the sound is some sort of deliberate interference.

She has to listen to the message three times, to make out everything he says. Sometimes his speech is slurred, sometimes it's fast and manic; sometimes his words trail off and when he starts speaking again it takes Brenna a moment to realize he's begun a new sentence.

He says, "I know I should have gotten in the car with you last night—I don't know why I didn't. Sometimes when I remember our fight by the car, it seems like I had good reasons for not going with you that I can't explain. Other times it feels like I wanted to get in and something was stopping me."

At another moment he'll say something which seems utterly contradictory, like, "I just feel like you're not giving Pearl a chance. She needs help, and I'm the one who has to help her. Can't you be a part of that with me? Besides, there's just something about her."

More than once, he says something like, "Brenna, I'm just confused. Please don't ask what's confusing me, I don't know how to answer that. But, please, if you can, come back up here."

By the time she's listened to the voicemail three times and pretty much deciphered it, she doesn't need to be asked again. Last night she thought he was simply being an asshole; mysteriously and uncharacteristically, sure, but that was all. Now, though, it's plain that something is really wrong with him. She should have stayed, she should have stayed when he

70

asked her to. She hangs up the phone, thinking to grab her keys and rush downstairs, call Mark on the way to her car.

After she hangs up she can still hear the rhythmic hissing swell of the sea.

She stands still. Dimly she hears the phone clatter on the floor. Her apartment is fading, she doesn't even think to say goodbye.

That hiss. The last thing she feels in her land-bound body is drool running down her chin from her half-open mouth. That static hiss of the sea is like millions of tiny gray-light fish flickering through and filling her body, as if the scrambled static scream of a television receiving no transmissions were a window into an electric sea.

The gray-light fish do nothing but flicker in and out of existence a million times per second, and bite. Their bites are not exactly hurting her yet, but she feels that they could. That it would require only a subtle adjustment in something's intention.

Child, says something.

Whatever it is, it's not that feminine voice she heard the other night, when she painted the tentacle and then wrote down her dream. It's the voice that spoke to her just before she awoke in the ocean, being rescued by Mark, the voice she hasn't been able to remember, but begins to recognize now.

Child, it says again.

And Brenna identifies it, with a terrified mental shout: *The Undersea King!*

With the thought she is overwhelmed by a roiling sensation, as if her spirit were being rocked back and forth in the tides; she has nothing she can quite locate as a body. Even though she feels not quite corporeal, she nevertheless knows at the same time that she is in water, and that it is by the grace of the Undersea King that she breathes.

In that lightless realm she sees before her a phosphorescent glow, a dim monstrous beast which is its own lamp. As it grows she realizes it is much further away than she believed, impossibly massive; it bears down on her, faster and faster, big as a town; she tries to scream, gargling soundless bubbles into the pressurized murk as the beast collides with her, and races through her a full five seconds, its impossible bulk passing through her like she was a dream. She emerges out its back end. Its tentacles still whipping at her back, she sees another monster just behind, bearing down on her. There's a relay of them, ramming her again and again, the vibrations of their noise thrumming through the dense water. The onslaught leaves Brenna stunned and she hangs stupidly there in the water, distantly wishing she had a body she could curl herself up in.

What I do to you in dream, I can do to you in life.

She is spinning round and round—she can feel it—but that seems impossible since the monsters are crashing through her one after another, as if they are moving in a straight line, as if she were nothing but a shadow on a busy freeway.

Had I not been tricked, says the King, *had the Hag not distracted me, I never would have let that headstrong foolish girl stray so far. Never, had my eye been upon her, would she have been allowed to strike so foolish a bargain. But now that it is done, I say she shall have what her silly, perfect, cruel heart desires. Neither my pride nor my love shall allow you to best her of it. She shall not turn to dead foam because she was unable to conquer a mere human heart, unable to defeat a rival such as yourself, a cow of what should be a matronly age.*

An unimaginable squeezing begins, pounding in upon each square centimeter of her astral form. Maybe Brenna would scream, if it were possible for her to make a sound in this state; but she wouldn't have the strength to expand her ribs with an intake of breath. Even so, she knows that the horrible pressure she feels is only a taste, that the Undersea King has only slightly relaxed whatever protective grip he holds her in. If he lets go altogether, she will wind up nothing more than a small raggedy flesh-purse filled with bone and gunk.

Stay away, the King says. *Release him to her. Stay away. Stay away.*

Stay away.

Those words, *stay away*, take on the pulse and rhythm of the surf. They fade gradually.

Brenna opens her eye to find herself back in her apartment—or maybe she didn't open her eyes, maybe they've been open all this time and it's just that now they've started seeing again.

As soon as she is fully back in the apartment, a wave of pain and nausea smashes into her, that puts her headache from the night before to shame. She collapses to the floor, already vomiting before her knees hit the linoleum. She quivers on the icy floor and pukes some more—draws her trembling pale hand up to wipe her mouth and when she pulls it away sees blood. A nosebleed. It's like she has the fucking bends, she thinks.

She lays there as long as it takes to somewhat recover. Then she forces herself up, peeling off her soiled clothes, and limps to the shower—she wrenched her knee when she fell. The shower is perfunctory, just enough to wash off the puke and the blood from her nose, and wake herself up a little. Once out, before even drying off, she limps back to her phone and calls Mark.

His voicemail picks up. Fuck that, she wants to talk to *him*; she disconnects and calls again. Again, the voicemail. This happens a couple times, till finally she gives in and leaves a voicemail.

"Mark, listen," she says, "I'm about to head to the emergency room. You have to do the same, baby. Take Holly along with you, and Pearl or whatever her name is…. I think Holly was right, Mark. That girl has something, some virus or something, and she passed it on to us. You've been acting funny, and me—well, I've been going through all sorts of stuff…. Anyway, we all have to get to the hospital right now, baby, all four of us. I would drive up there and go with you but I don't trust myself to make the trip, I'm just going to go around the block to Coney Island Hospital."

She's about to end the message there. But she thinks twice, and says, "Call me. Call and let me know when you hear this, and that you're on your way to the hospital. Trust me, Mark. I just listened to your message and there's, there's something off about you. And I just had something crazy happen to me. We're infected with something, and it has to do with that girl."

It's hard to stop talking, she feels driven to keep blabbering until she knows for sure he's grasped what she's saying. But she's said everything she has to say. Except one thing: "I love you," she adds, and grabs her keys and leaves the apartment.

But as she's limping down the stairs she keeps wondering what might happen if Mark doesn't take her message seriously. Or maybe for some reason he won't hear it. Or maybe he will hear it, but the weird oceanic brain fever that keeps fucking with her and that seems to have addled him will have pushed him so far that he won't be able to understand what she's talking about.

Or say that Mark does go to the hospital, that he takes Holly and the waif along, that they're all fine, but that she's not able to know that for sure because she's in a different hospital and they've, say, taken her phone away for some reason. Even that would be too maddening to accept.

Making her way to her car, she calls Mark again. Again, his voicemail—goddammit! "All right," she says, "I'm coming up there. I'm coming up there to make sure you go to the doctor. But do not wait for me. Go as soon as you hear this message—just leave me a note, to let me know. Or call me. I'll follow you to whatever hospital you're at.... I'm serious, Mark." She hangs up as she arrives at her car.

Inside, the key about to slide into the ignition, she hesitates. Gathers her thoughts. Collects her breath.

Is it safe for her to drive?

The short answer is, "No." She keeps on having weird visions where she feels like she's left her body. During one of these she apparently wandered into the sea. If that happens while she's driving she could die, or kill someone. Really, she ought to call an ambulance.

"But," she tells herself, "those things only happened when I was painting, or when I heard the sea. Or, almost, when I was meditating."

Later it will hit her what an insane, nonsensical piece of reasoning that is, and it will frighten her that she found it convincing enough to stake her life on. Right now, though, it seems perfectly natural. She also has an idea she might be particularly prone to the seizures, or whatever, if she were asleep. Painting, listening to the sea, meditation, and sleeping: those trance-like states.

"So I'll stay alert," she says aloud. Talking to herself, to stay focussed. She turns the key in the ignition, not trying to fight the butterflies in her stomach, but using them to keep herself frosty. "I'll stay the fuck alert and keep my eyes on the road."

She pulls away from the curb, and is on her way to Long Beach to fetch Mark and take him to the hospital.

Ten

By the time she gets to Long Beach and is approaching George's and Albert's house, Brenna is starting to wonder if driving won't turn out to have been a fatally bad idea, after all. She imagines that this is what driving drunk must be like, the constant wearying effort of fixing her attention on the road and on all the manual tasks that are usually automatic. Like if she had to remember how to breathe every time she took a breath. Several times a billboard or a patch of sky or a passing car will catch her attention, and it's all she can do to keep her gaze on the road. All the while, she has the feeling that someone is tugging at the sleeve of her mind, trying to get her to look elsewhere: either someplace inward, or at the passing scenery. But she refuses.

To keep herself focussed, she decides to recite "Stopping By Woods On a Snowy Evening" again. But two lines in she realizes that reciting the poem is more likely to lull her into a trance than anything else. So she starts piecing it together in reverse. Haltingly, slowly, she enunciates the poem backwards: "Sleep, I, before, to ... no, I mean go ... go, to ... um ... miles ... and...." That requires enough concentration to stave off whatever is trying to happen in her mind.

By the time she pulls onto George's and Albert's street, she has a headache. It's from a combination of whatever the main problem is, and the mental gymnastics of reciting that poem backwards twice. While she's still a couple of blocks away, she sees Holly shuffling along the side of the road in her T-shirt and shorts. She's barefoot, without even her flip-flops, and is walking on the grass instead of the hot pavement. Her head hangs and she is crying, not even bothering to cover her face with her hands.

Brenna stops the car and leans over to open the door. "Holly, what's wrong? Get in the car."

Holly stops, but makes no move to get in the car. She looks down at Brenna with her red slick face, her mouth twisted in on itself like a wounded animal. She says, "I don't know what it is with that girl."

"What?" Brenna's worried that maybe everyone is more damaged than she'd thought. "Why do you say that?"

"He *yelled* at me," says Holly. "Mark *yelled* at me. I've never seen him like that. I wasn't even saying anything to that fucking Pearl bitch when he did it. He just came up on me and got in my face and was like, Pearl is going through a really hard transition right now and she doesn't need us giving her shit."

Sour dread seeps all through Brenna's body. "A 'transition'?" she says. "What does that mean?"

Holly doesn't answer the question, but says, "And he told me that I should be worried about you, instead of him and Pearl. He said it like he was really mad, or like you were in trouble or something. He said, 'Brenna's the one who's in trouble, so why don't you go worry about her right now.' What does that even mean?"

"I don't know. Get in the car, Holly."

Holly shakes her head.

"Holly, quit screwing around. Get in the car, please."

Again, Holly shakes her head. "Naw," she says, shoulders slumped, looking at the ground in utter sadness. "Naw, I'm not gonna do that. I'm just gonna walk around." She turns over her shoulder to send a dark look back at George's and Albert's. "And then I'm gonna go have a showdown with that bitch once and for all."

It's no use trying to get Holly in the car. Brenna wants to hurry and get to the house. What Holly's said freaks her out even more. Brenna believes her, but at the same time she can't quite imagine Mark acting that way.

As she drives the rest of the way to George's and Albert's, she notices that she can hear the surf. She once again starts reciting her Frost backwards.

All during the drive, she's vacillated between trying to keep tabs on her state of mind, and trying not to think about it at all, for fear it'll lead her down strange pathways. As she gets out of the car, though, as the sound of the sea comes to her unmuffled by the engine noise, she can't shake the weird feeling she has of it as some kind of presence. She doesn't even know what she means by that. Whenever she sees that cliché tossed around in a sci-fi or fantasy book or movie, whenever someone says "I feel a presence," she scoffs. But here she is, with the day offering her yet another chance to be humbled; because it turns out to be possible after all.

And the intention of that presence is subtly different from the previous incarnations. There's a gloating quality to it. And a beckoning one, as if the ocean itself were wagging an invisible finger at her to come into the house. Without really noticing that she's begun thinking of them as genuine personages, Brenna tries to decide if this beckoning presence is the Undersea King or the Old Witch. The Undersea King, she thinks, though there's less grandeur in him now. He seems almost gleeful.

Despite the fact that she risked her life to drive all the way here from Coney Island, it makes her not want to go into the house.

But she knows that's bullshit, and that she's got to suck it up. She raises her hand to knock—but then, something stops her. It occurs to her that maybe it would be better to be discreet. As if she were worried that there might be something inside, that it would be best not to alert. That makes no sense, she'll realize later—the whole point of being here is to get Mark, as well as Holly and the waif, so it's no use being secretive about it.

She opens the door. No one is there in the front room. Although it's bright outside, the house seems more shadowy than ever. Brenna creeps inside.

The air inside seems moist. It has a tangy smell.

She catches herself acting as if she's sneaking in, instead of grabbing Mark and leaving with the same urgency with which she drove up here. She makes herself say his name: "Mark?" She intended for it to be a cry, but it comes out hushed, her voice cracking on the word.

Something pushes her to walk upstairs. No, that's impossible; nothing could have "pushed" her; she simply decided on her own to go up there, for whatever reason. As she moves along the upstairs hallway, she begins to hear a slapping sound, a light one, like sped-up wavelets breaking on a rocky shore.

As she nears the source of the slapping sound that tangy, briny smell grows stronger.

There's a door ajar ahead. Brenna knows it's the bedroom from when Mark gave her the tour. She's never been inside it, just stood on the threshold—that was where, according to the plan, she would have slept with Mark. Her pace slows and grows more and more reluctant as she nears the open doorway, because that eerie, gloating mockery grows ever thicker in the air. It's a physical effort to move her feet forward, as if she's having to drag them through a current.

The light from that room is clearer than elsewhere in the house. She can see that before she gets all the way there. It has a bluish quality, as if the sunlight is filtered through a blue gauze curtain.

She steps into the doorway and remembers in a rush that the whole reason for coming up here is that she's losing her mind. Because what she's seeing is a hallucination.

The waif is on top of Mark in George's and Albert's bed, he's fucking her. Gripping her by the hips as he stares awestruck up at her; she straddles him, her torso regal and erect. For Brenna it feels like she's having an out-of-body experience; the sight of Mark prone and fucking is familiar to her, but never from this vantage point, never from all the way across a room. The bottoms of his feet are facing her. How often has she seen the soles of his feet while making love? Not during any ordinary sessions, that's for sure.

It is a hallucination. This isn't something Brenna thinks in order to protect herself, this is simply her default assumption. She notices the slight jiggle of the firm flesh of the waif's small round bouncing ass, and frowns; that seems an oddly prosaic detail for her mind to supply for a hallucination.

Still riding Mark, the waif turns her neck at what seems an impossible angle to look at Brenna. She clearly already knows Brenna is there. She locks eyes with her and Brenna realizes that this isn't a hallucination, it's actually physically happening. The waif's gaze is swollen with triumph, disdain, victory. Brenna recognizes it, but from someplace deep below the level of her lived experience, from some hard-wired primordial memory; the waif's expression is not one that any civilized person has ever worn.

Brenna must have made some sort of noise, because now Mark's eyes have snapped open. His gaze is filled first with incomprehension, then horror. "Brenna!" he says, and starts trying to move Pearl off of him. She maintains her seat despite his bucking, like he's a horse she's breaking.

Brenna takes a step back.

Mark finally manages to toss the waif aside. "Brenna, wait," he says, jumping out of bed.

Brenna runs from the room, as if he's an enemy. Races through the hall, down the stairs, through the living room. Holly's come back inside; her eyes widen at the sight of Brenna and she starts to ask a question, but Brenna shoves her out of the way and bursts out the front door.

"Brenna!" Mark's right behind her, chasing her. She fumbles for her keys, skidding to a stop in front of her car. He grabs her arm, tries to turn her around. "Brenna, wait...."

"Let go of me!" He's naked, she sees. In her peripheral vision she notices an older guy standing a few lawns down, staring at them.

She pushes back on Mark's chest. That roaring is back, that feeling like she's inside a huge roaring conch. It's so loud she has trouble hearing him: "Brenna, wait, I love you, we can talk about this...."

"The fuck *off* of me!" He lets her go—later, she'll recall the confusion on his face as he does so, wondering if it's the proper thing. Quicker than he could have expected, she spins around and slips into her car, tries to slam the door behind her.

He grabs the door. "Brenna, wait, please...."

"Let go of the door! Let it go or I'll break your fucking hand!"

Reluctantly, he does let go. She slams it, almost hard enough to break the door handle. He's still talking to her as she gets the key in the ignition and starts the car. She can't make out what he says, even though the thin pane of glass shouldn't be enough to muffle his voice. It's like he's speaking from underwater.

Brenna pulls out. It doesn't even occur to her to watch out for Mark's toes, but luckily he jumps out of the way. She speeds off, in her rage and panic forgetting all about the visions and the hospital.

Despite that, she does once again have that sense of a presence. But no longer a seductive or a threatening one. Now it's like she feels mocking, jeering laughter being silently barked at her.

And why shouldn't she hear that? Is she not an idiot? Wasn't she so willfully blind to what was going on that she imagined some big crazy conspiracy, rather than simply acknowledge that Mark wanted to fuck that little blonde waif? She'd actually preferred to give herself hallucinations, to drive herself literally insane, rather than let herself see what any gossipy teenage girl would have picked up on.

And she had thought she was so sensible. So free and liberal. She's always said that she and Mark are both free to walk any time they feel they're not getting what they need. Yet here she is, as crushed as any spurned little girlie. She rides the blinding white wave of fury out of the neighborhood.

After two minutes of speeding away, it's already getting hard to maintain that fury, though. She needs the solid structure of it to keep herself going. Knowing she's about to lose her grasp on it, she turns into the parking lot of a shopping center. It's a big blue expanse and not a busy day; she drives to an isolated spot near the back of the lot and parks, turns off the ignition, and finally, as desperate whimpers escape her, she clambers over the seat and makes it to the back just before everything comes bubbling out of her.

There's a beach towel back there; without worrying about when it was last washed or what it's been used for since, she stuffs it into her mouth. Now she has something to bite and scream into, and something to muffle her sobs. Curled up, hidden and silent in the back of the car, she has her breakdown in private.

Who knows how long she's there. She doesn't care. At last her weeping physically exhausts her enough that she returns to something like calm. She still continues to lie in the backseat. Twice she hears groups of cheerful voices pass by very near, and she holds her breath, but they never peek into the car and notice her.

Brenna makes herself breathe steadily. It's all right. Everything ends and sometimes that hurts. But she'll ride it out and it will be all right.

She wipes her face on the dirty towel and climbs back into the front seat. Checks and sees that she has indeed been here long enough for the quality of the sunlight to change.

Almost unwillingly, she checks her phone. As always, the ringer is off. Both Mark and Holly have called, Holly three times and Mark eight. Both have left multiple messages.

No one else has called. But then again, Brenna thinks with a hollow feeling, who else does she know? It seems to her right now that she knows nobody. Just casual acquaintances.

She sits there a while, slumped over. This is a sad feeling. A death feeling. But it's not one that will keep her from driving, the way the other one was, that one she had to ride out in the backseat. So she turns the key in the ignition once again, and turns on the engine, and pulls the car out of the parking space and begins her trek back to Coney Island.

Eleven

Back in her apartment, she wanders. Starts in the kitchen nook, not cooking, not eating. Walks across the room. Goes back and opens her tiny closet, though she's not looking for anything. There's an old, empty kitty-litter box gathering dust. Brenna used to have a cat, but he died. Now she supposes that maybe she'll get another one.

That painting from the other night, of the maelstrom, still rests facing the wall. During the drive she decided to look at it again, now that she knows what was really making her crazy. But she leaves it where it is. And she's still scared to paint, and too rattled to read.

Basically she just hangs around the apartment, waiting for it to get dark so she can have an excuse to go to bed. Finally, it does. This is the third night since the waif arrived—tomorrow will be the third day.

Unlike the night before, she doesn't use a night-light. She doesn't care anymore.

Mark and Holly have left dozens of text messages. Lying on her cot, the screen of the phone her only light, Brenna deletes all the texts unread. She doesn't want them filling her inbox. Brenna turns the phone off and slips it under her cot. She lies down, straight as if she were in a coffin, gazing up into the darkness.

She starts to cry, snuffling and sputtering. That's okay. In the darkness, there's no one to see, no one to hide from.

It seems unthinkable that she will ever go to sleep. But eventually the habits of the body start to take over. She begins to have woozy moments which she thinks must be times when she dozed off.

There in the darkness it begins to seem she can make out flickers of refracted light, filtering down. Then she realizes that she's seeing this with eyes more subtle than the balls in her head. The blue darkness has grown warmer, she's cushioned in mid-air by an invisible swell.

Again, there's that sense of a presence. It takes her a long time to identify this one as the Undersea King, so different is his mood than it was during all prior visitations. No more jeering; no more threats. Perhaps it feels a bit akin to that first message, when he tried to drown her, but this time Brenna senses no intention to hypnotize, to harm.... In this sleeping state, Brenna has forgotten that she does not believe in the Undersea King.

He wants to bring her comfort. It's quite generous, by his standards. *Sleep*, he tells her. He makes her know that he is fond of her—rarely has he seen a mortal with such spirit. He puts into her mind the knowledge of his gratitude to her for having relinquished her claim to his daughter's prize. The King knew his child would triumph, and yet a father cannot help but worry and then feel relief. By giving up the human, Brenna has earned the gratitude of the King. By not doing it out of fear of himself, she has earned his regard. He makes her know that, to show that gratitude, regard, and fondness, he would be willing to bring her down below to be his concubine.

She recoils so violently that she nearly wakes up.

Very well, very well! She need not fear that she will be forced. The King is not his daughter. He has learned the bitter lesson that some pleasures cannot be forced—he has had time to learn it. But she shall have a boon. Go on, ask a boon, whatever she likes. He will enjoy demonstrating to her his might and scope.

Brenna keeps her proud gaze turned up, towards the flickering lights, and away from the voice's source, someplace in the dark depths below. The only boon she would care to ask is that they go back in time, and prevent the waif from ever arriving at all. If the King could do that, he already would have.

So be it, the King tells her. She is proud to the point of foolishness, but that pride is what is pleasing to him. He would not break her spirit needlessly—mortals have such a brief span in which to flower.

But if she will not ask a boon, he will grant her one. On one condition: that Brenna will not try to stop his daughter from coming into possession of the mortal man's heart. If, when his child's knell rings on the morrow, Brenna has not prevented that from being so, then the Undersea King gives her his word: she shall never die in the sea.

It may seem a small and silly thing. But the Undersea King has taken many, many human lives; and only rarely has he altogether renounced his claim to one.

He is releasing his hold on her, letting her drift back up. But now, at last, her pride spurs her to address him. She works her way back down, just far enough to tell the King not to worry about that; never has she tried to insinuate herself into anyone's heart, and never will she; if Mark wants Pearl, he can have her, she won't stoop to squabbling over a man who can't make up his mind whether he wants her, himself.

The King chuckles. Ah, he tells her, for a female she is very formidable. Very well, then; even if the mortal man does prove fickle to his headstrong beloved, the King's boon will still remain watertight, so long as the mortal doesn't betray the child thanks to Brenna's machinations.

The very idea that she would go angling for Mark's affection galls her, and now that she's been roused she tries to swim down after the King, determined to give him a piece of her mind. But he ignores her angry hails, and no matter how obstinately she swims, those waters are too dark and dense for her to be able to follow him. She's willing to bet he hears her calls, but he slips away anyhow, arrogantly uninterested now that he's said what he wanted.

All she accomplishes is to thrash around enough that she wakes up, gasping her eyes open in the dark. She stares around, blind and disoriented, exhausted as if she'd just gone on a very long journey. *Remember the dream!*, she tells herself. *Remember the dream!* Then she falls back down into sleep.

She sleeps hard, for fourteen hours. Wakes up much later than usual. A bit after noon. The apartment is baking with all the sunlight invading it. She opens a window, wishing she'd closed the blackout curtains last night before bed.

Then again, fuck that. It's good to have all this sunlight. It's good to chase out the gloom.

The vision of Mark and the waif fucking stabs her in the temples, from the inside. She has to stop and put her hands on her head.

Something is nagging at her, something she's supposed to remember. Only in the shower does last night's dream come back to her. She stands a long time under the water, as if entranced, staring at the wall and remembering the gratitude of the Undersea King.

So she's still having hallucinations, she thinks grimly as she scrubs herself dry. Of course, all dreams are hallucinations, but these are different. Well. Just means she's upset by the events of yesterday. She'll be having strange dreams a long, long time. Till she dies, probably.

Out in the living room, she gets dressed. Looking at the back of that canvas she's still afraid to face out. What galls her about the dream is the fucking gratitude. As if she has deferred to the Undersea King, as if she has given up on Mark because it complies with the King's wishes, and not because of him fucking someone else while being an asshole. That is total bullshit, and she would love the chance to set the Undersea King straight.

Brenna has to remind herself that there is no Undersea King. She made him up.

Even so, it pisses her off.

She walks to her cot. Bends down and takes the phone out from under it, looks at its blank screen. She would rather start planning her day—better to stay in the apartment, or go out?—but feels like she won't be able to till after she's faced the deluge of messages she's bound to have from Mark. Even if it's only to erase them.

Or maybe there won't be any. After all, the Mark she's known for five years wouldn't beg and plead and push and crowd. Sobering, that it takes so little time for her to begin thinking of him as someone who would do just that. This degradation of her interior image of him suddenly seems the cruelest cut of all, crueler even than the sight of him fucking the waif.

Either way. Whether he left a hundred messages, or not a single one, it seems like she ought to know. Without noticing she holds her breath, and presses the power button on her phone.

The phone takes several seconds to warm up. Brenna's plan was to walk around the apartment while that happened, do stuff. Instead she winds up riveted to the phone, watching it and waiting for it to boil.

And it does. Once it's awake and its reception is on, she watches it blink like a Christmas tree as it registers message after message after message. Most of them are from Mark, a few are, again, from Holly. Voicemails, text messages. One pops up from one of Brenna's private yoga clients and for a moment she's discombobulated, wondering what it's doing in the mix.

Finally they're all done. She has more than fifty fucking messages. Brenna walks away from the phone, leaving it on her cot with a mixture of disgust and fear.

As she cooks herself breakfast, she thinks about how it's odd that Holly should be calling so much, too. But it's not, really. She's probably freaked out and trying to figure out what's going on—although if she were that freaked out, she could just get in her car and drive back to Philly. Probably she's salivating at the hope of bagging Mark right out from under the waif's nose, and is trying to confirm that Mark and Brenna are really finished as a salve to her conscience.

Sliding her eggs onto her plate, she sees the phone lighting up yet again. Jesus. She's not even going to look at it, she tells herself. But then before she sits down to eat she does walk back to the cot, just to see who it is. Since she started cooking she's gotten five new messages, four from Holly and then the last one from Mark. She puts the phone back down on the cot. If it were only Holly calling and texting Brenna would answer, because she'd be afraid something had happened to Mark. But as long as they're both well enough to keep bothering her, she doesn't need to know anything else about them.

She sits down to her eggs. In spite of everything, her appetite doesn't fail her; she's famished. As if she went on a long strenuous journey last night.

As she chews her eggs she tries not to brood. Tries not to see Pearl straddling Mark as he pumps away at her: yeah, right, that'll work.

It's weird that Holly keeps calling so much. Brenna's still sure that she's only calling because she wants to try to fuck Mark and wants to hear that Brenna's through with him so that she won't have to feel bad. But, still, that she would call this much? Isn't it odd?

In the middle of eating her eggs she goes back to the cot and picks up the phone. There's another text message, from Mark. Brenna actually wavers for a second.... But no, she doesn't *want* to check that message. She puts the phone back on the cot, face-down again, and goes back to finish her eggs.

By the time she's doing the dishes it's well after two. Jesus. Where did the day go? Brenna pauses in her dishwashing—no, really, where did it go? She tries to tally up what little she's done so far today, figures out how long each item took. It doesn't seem possible she's been awake for more than two hours.

Well. Time acts funny during the first day of a break-up....

Those unread, unheard messages keep nagging at her. If she listens to them, she'll only feel even worse. What she ought to do is go erase them all.

Now she asks herself if maybe she's scared to read and listen to them.

She frowns. *Is* that why? What has she got to be scared of? And yet something about the idea rings true.

She remembers the condescending gratitude of the Undersea King the night before. It would be too much if he thinks she's scared, to boot.

Plus, is there some truly bad thing she's afraid of, that might have happened? Or might be about to happen? That she could still stop?

She marches back to the cot and picks up the phone. Hits the button to look at the text messages.

A few minutes later she's heading downstairs, still scrolling through the nearly seventy text messages. They don't make much sense but their cumulative effect is so distressing that by the time she leaves the building she's running. She tries to call Holly and Mark as she gets in her car, but now all of a sudden they're apparently nowhere near their phones.

The particular text that grows more and more ominous in her mind is one that at first only confused her. It's the last one Mark sent: HELP, I CAN'T LEAVE.

Twelve

Again and again Brenna tries calling the two of them, breaking her own rule about never talking on the phone while driving. They won't pick up. It unnerves her so much she starts to get angry, again. They've been calling her for, what, nineteen hours, and now they can't pick up the phone? Hopefully they're just messing with her—but maybe something bad has happened.

Rather than call the police (because, as it stands, she has little to say; it's not so odd that her cheating boyfriend wouldn't return her calls), she starts cycling through her messages.

They don't make a lot of sense. Some of Mark's are diatribes about how unfair Brenna's being to the waif. Some are pleas for her to return to the house, declarations that it's Brenna he truly loves. Several times he announces that he's about to head down to her apartment, but then in his next message the subject will be dropped. He exhibits all the characteristics she emphatically does *not* associate with him, or at least she didn't three days ago: paranoia, weakness, pettiness, whininess. She doesn't exactly hold it against him, because now she knows something strange is going on. But still.

She's not going up there to get him back from the waif—if he really wants her, he can have her. If he can manage to decide one way or the other. She just wants to make sure he's okay.

In the rearview mirror she notices that the paint stains have nearly faded from her head.

By the time she gets to George's and Albert's, the sky has begun to hint at dusk. Brenna gets out of her car. It's preternaturally quiet—no sounds of the neighbors, or even the eternal ubiquitous music of distant traffic. Only the surf, unseen from this vantage point but filling the world nonetheless.

"Hello?" she calls, without knowing why she doesn't simply go to the front door. There's no answer.

She makes herself walk up the lawn, up to the front porch. The door is slightly ajar. Brenna hesitates, taps it lightly so that it drifts further open. "Hello?" she calls again. "Mark? Holly?" Then: "Pearl?"

It's weird that no one answers. Mark's and Holly's vehicles are still here, after all. Maybe the waif is a psychopathic killer. But probably not. They probably all got drunk and passed out, or something like that.

Brenna slips through the crack in the door, into the shadowed house.

All the lights are out. The curtains are drawn but the sun still filters in. The place is messy. There are empty cans everywhere, seafood cans. Brenna thinks they must have left to go shopping, at least, but on the kitchen counter she sees a receipt for shitloads of seafood, dated today, and it includes a fee for delivery.

By now she's become aware of a slurping sound from the living room. She steps in there and sees the waif, completely naked, kneeling on the floor and licking the last contents of a tuna can. She must have figured out the can opener. There's blood on her hands from where she cut herself on something. Worse, her fucking mouth is covered in blood. Brenna winces in disgust—the waif must have cut her lips and tongue on the sharp edges of a can, and now doesn't even care enough to clean herself. On the floor next to her is a ripped-open styrofoam package, and within and around it are scattered bones of fish, with tatters of flesh still attached. Has the waif taken the fish out of the package and eaten it raw?

Ever since Brenna stepped into the room the waif's glare has been fixed on her. She heard Brenna in the kitchen.

Brenna knows that it's no use asking this creature anything, but she still tries: "Where are Mark and Holly?"

Sure enough, the waif only glowers at her in reply.

Brenna turns her gaze upstairs. That was the last place she saw Mark, when she caught him fucking the waif. She turns towards it, puts a foot on the first step, then the second. Fights the urge to turn and see if the waif is watching. Brenna knows she is—she can feel the waif's eyes on her back.

The stairs don't creak or anything. It's a well-kept house. The only sound remains the sea. Brenna tries to ignore it.

At the top of the stairs she hesitates. "Mark?" she says again. There's still no answer.

Why won't he answer?

She makes herself step forward. To the bedroom. This door, too, is ajar. Brenna stops and nudges it the rest of the way open, holding her breath and squinting as if she might once again see Mark and the waif fucking, even though she knows the waif is downstairs, stuffing her face.

There's no one in this room. The bed is empty. Unmade, rumpled.

Brenna moves back out into the hall. "Mark?"

She comes to the bathroom door. It's closed. Gently, she raps on it. "Mark?" she says. There's no answer. She knocks again. "Mark?" Nothing. She puts her hand on the knob. "Mark, if you're in there, heads up, I'm coming in."

Nothing. She purses her lips and opens the door.

It's like yesterday, when she saw Mark and the waif fucking, it's the same shock of impossibility, only it's worse this time. Brenna stands blinking and gaping down at the tub, wondering why Mark appears from such a funny angle—then she thinks it must be a two-dimensional open-eyed image of Mark, a life-size nude photo that someone bizarrely placed at the bottom of the tub—then she realizes that the angle is due to the refraction of the light, he's under water, the tub is full, the water is still, as if he's not moved in a very long time.

"Mark!" she screams, and throws herself to her knees, plunging her arms into the water to pull him out. *"Mark!"*

Miraculously, he's alive. He splutters, spits out a lot of water, but seems unharmed. "Brenna," he says.

Brenna nearly weeps with relief, but clamps herself back under control. "What were you doing?" she demands.

He gets that new look she hates, that confused look. "She told me to practice."

Okay, whatever. "How long were you under that water?"

"A long time. For a long time, I think."

"For a long time, you think," growls Brenna. She rises to her feet, nearly falling over because she fucked her knee up even worse lunging down like that beside the tub. "Stay here," she orders Mark, and starts to leave, then doubles back to flip the drain and release the water from the tub. "Do *not* do that again," she tells Mark, sternly.

She limps back down the hall to the stairs, moving fast, ignoring the pain in her leg as best she can. As she descends she sees the waif, still naked, blood on her hands and mouth, glaring up at her.

"Get your clothes on, bitch, we're going to the doctor," Brenna says, and limps past her. "Holly!" she shouts. It won't surprise her if the waif winds up having to be wrangled into the car, in which case she'll need help. "Holly!"

Brenna's heading out the back to see if Holly's down at the water, but suddenly the offensiveness of the waif's scowl hits her, on a delayed reaction. She marches back to the waif and grabs her by the bloody face, pinching her cheeks between her thumb and fingers and forcing her jaw open the way an infuriated adult might do with a stubborn child. "Listen to me, you stupid fucking kid. Have you ever built something? Built *anything*? Do you know what it means to build a relationship over five years? You think you can march in here and take that over in three days, with nothing but your bouncy tits and your cutesy smile? Well, you can't. Because you're nothing. You're not shit. You're a spoiled fucking princess who hasn't had to become anything yet and who's so lazy she never will. You are at most a fucking trip for men to take that they can send a pretty postcard of to their buddies back home. You may be able to fuck shit up but you will never be able to keep anything because you are *not ... fucking ... shit.*"

The waif screams. Brenna jumps back, snatching away her hand like the waif's head is on fire. For a moment Brenna stands there, breathing hard, staring in terror; that wailing, shrieking, moaning, furious scream can't be a natural sound. There must be a machine attached to the waif, a microphone with effects hidden in her throat. The waif's eyes stay fixed on Brenna as she screams. There's a pause as she draws breath for a second shriek. That breaks the spell, and Brenna whirls away from her, once more heading for the back door. "Holly!"

She caroms out onto the back porch and comes to a halt. Yet another sight she can't register, that seems to have come from outside reality. There, on its back on the porch, is what looks like Holly. Mouth open, open eyes blind to the sky. Most of her throat is missing, a jagged red hole. Red all down her shirt, she's lying in a pool of red. Brenna looks down at her own hand, at the blood that got on it when she grabbed the waif's face. The horrible scream from inside mixes with the roar of the waves.

Mark—she has to get Mark, and then they can get the fuck out of here. She looks around for a weapon and doesn't see one—grabs a medium-sized flowerpot in lieu of anything better. It's heavy enough to hurt if it got smashed into someone's face.

She edges back inside, holding that ridiculous flowerpot, keeping her eyes locked on the waif. "Mark!" she cries. The waif hisses at her.

Mark comes hurrying down the stairs. He's put on underwear this time, but hasn't paused to dry off and is still wet.

"Grab your keys and get in your truck and go, Mark!" she calls. "She's psycho, she killed Holly."

"*What?*" says Mark. Before either he or Brenna can do anything more, the waif picks up an end table and throws it at him, with another of her animal howls. It's a direct hit, it knocks him down.

"Mark!" screams Brenna, rushing towards him, not stopping to wonder how the tiny waif managed to hurl that table. She tosses the flowerpot at the waif and misses.

Before Brenna can get to Mark, the waif leaps in front of her with a yowl. Brenna would shove her out of the way, or try to, but instead she stops cold; the waif's eyes have turned to black orbs, like a shark's.

Brenna takes a step back. Now both legs are shaky.

Again the waif roars. She's gotten back *a* voice, anyway: that trumpet of doom the Witch gave her. Brenna realizes that the waif's time is up.

Almost up, anyway. She might still have a few moments left for Brenna.

Brenna makes another dash for Mark, but the waif's foot jumps in front of her, blocking the way. It smashes through the floorboards, sending a hail of dust and splinters rocketing into Brenna's face. She looks over in amazement to see if the waif has crumpled in agony, her foot broken. But there's no pain in the waif's face, only fury. And how did her leg stretch so far? It's about five feet longer than it ought to be. The flesh looks taut, yet it quivers and bubbles. And is turning brown.

Brenna looks back at the waif, not at her face but her lower half. Everything from the waist down is bubbling and morphing. Her right leg is still standing normally on the floor, but her left one is extended far away, at an angle, punched through the floorboards. Suddenly it begins racing around towards Brenna, tearing through the wooden floor like it was water, leaving in its wake a trough shattering through the wood, spraying splinters and sawdust.

Brenna dances out of the way. She sees Mark is stirring. Brenna can't get to him right now, the waif is between them. Besides, she thinks she can tell from the waif's glare that Mark isn't her target.

She turns to the staircase. Clambers up the stairs. Up, away from the writhing black bubbling thing. If she stays downstairs it will easily kill her, but though her brain can't encompass its shape it looks like nothing that could climb stairs. First time in her life, she tries to scream for help, finds she can't; the hiccuppy breath gets caught in her throat.

There are noises of tearing, crashing, ripping, roars of random percussion. Brenna feels the staircase slipping and collapsing underneath her, despite everything is level-headed enough to know the sensation is probably nothing but the dizziness of her own terror. But no, the staircase is indeed collapsing under her. She doesn't look back.

She scrambles onto the landing at the last moment, as the structure dissolves underneath her, her feet nearly slipping off the edge. Upstairs bathroom—where the fuck is it?! Even though she was just there, she's almost too freaked out to remember. That door should have a lock. Luckily the room she pops into is the right one. Hurls herself inside, forces her shaking hands to lock the door.

Brenna backs against the wall. The window's open but too small to crawl through—anyway, she's too high. That door won't hold long but help will come soon. She tries to scream again but still can't control her breath. But any scream would be superfluous in this monstrous racket, would be swallowed in the destruction of the house. Everything shakes as the foundations are jostled. People must be running to investigate, to rescue.

Not only is there noise, there's also a smell. There's a rich, fetid, rotting smell, sweetish under the brack, getting stronger; overpowering, approaching.

She stares at the bathroom door. Again the house shakes with the wrath of the creature. Can it be mangling Holly's corpse downstairs, in its fury? Brenna reminds herself that it can't get to her. Her fear of it bursting through that door is fear-addled insanity. With the staircase destroyed, it can't climb up.

It might tear the house down and bring her to it. But it cannot ascend to her.

She's telling herself that as a black thing bursts through the door like a hydraulic ram. Chips fly into her face as she screams.

The tentacle whips and bangs around, obliterating the door. Brenna screams involuntarily, a weak, shrill sound—if that thing whacks her it'll kill her.

The tentacle slams right past Brenna; she yelps and cowers away from it, but realizes through the dust and noise that it has knocked out the exterior wall she was pushing back against a moment before. She leans forward, afraid to go tumbling into empty space.

Like a stupid blind animal in its own right, the tentacle wraps around the exposed floor beam and all the slack goes out of the musculature. Maybe the waif is still downstairs, and trying to haul her new mass up to the second floor.

Or maybe she's trying to tear the second floor down, which exactly what she's accomplishing. The floor tilts; Brenna nearly falls backwards, but manages to ride the slipping surface almost all the way down. At the last moment she's thrown clear, out through the ruined wall onto the ground, just before the ceiling would have crashed down and buried her in rubble.

Brenna forces herself up, barely feeling her knee anymore. Races down to the sea, not yet turning to look at the destruction she hears being wrought behind her.

Once the waves don't seem too far away she does turn to look. Pieces of the destroyed house buckle, slide, and are thrown aloft as the monster's gelatinous, hydraulic mass tries to work itself loose. Brenna doesn't see Mark. She prays he's all right.

She keeps turning from the ocean to look over her shoulder, even though she knows she shouldn't look back—not least because it slows her running. Now she sees the waif finally work herself free. From the waist up, she's still basically the waif, although she still has those black eyes and Brenna thinks there's something funny about her mouth, it's twisted, bigger, it's stuffed with fangs.

Her vast lower part is the massive tentacled sea creature.

The waif turns her head Brenna's way. Brenna thinks she's been spotted—that's confirmed when the waif lets out a roar of rage and triumph. She sends her tentacles jutting out of the wreckage and starts scuttling towards Brenna on those prehensile cords of muscle, coming ten feet a step.

Brenna turns back to face forward. Only a few more paces to the sea. *Hey King, I kept my word, didn't I? Is it my fault if Mark didn't fall in love with her, after all?*

Her feet splash through the waves. She makes herself run fast, despite the drag of the tide and the weight of her sodden shoes. With impossible effort, she raises her knees as she runs until the water's too high to get her feet out. A wave comes, she dives under it. She's in maybe five feet of water now. Starts swimming again, desperate to get to deeper water, to make it as hard as possible for the waif to pull her out and kill her on the shore—if what the Witch said was true, she's only got to stay alive a few minutes, at most.

But the waif has her. Brenna feels the vise of a tentacle around her calf, yanking her back. She can't help but scream—her face is underwater when she does, and in screaming she loses the air she was holding and chokes on a gulp of seawater.

The waif flips her onto her back. For a second Brenna sees the sunlight breaking on the waves above, then the waif's new bulk eclipses the sight. Tentacles wrap around her neck, her arm, the other leg, and around her torso. They squeeze her, grinding her down into the sandy shifting bottom. The waif rests her nether bulk upon Brenna's face and chest, rubbing it against her, crushing her between two unyielding pressures.

Through her terror Brenna notices that she's not dead. She doesn't feel the all-bursting sensation that she imagines comes with suffocation and drowning. Somehow, there's breath in her throat, in her lungs. She can't exactly locate it, or guess how she's taken it in, or quite explain the sensation to herself. But she knows it's real. The proof is that she's alive.

She becomes aware that the pressure of the waif's body on her face and chest is lightening. At first she thinks that's because the waif is quitting out of boredom, or floating away. Then she realizes that the waif's body offers less resistance, because it's dissolving. She feels it rubbing back and forth against both of her cheeks now, as if her face has worn a furrow in it.

Then the tentacles are soft enough that, though they're still heavy, Brenna's struggle is enough to break them apart. She kicks off from the bottom, her lungs bursting. Now that she doesn't need his help to survive anymore, the King has taken back that spare breath he lent her.

She breaks the surface of the water in the middle of a patch of oily brown foam. Its stench nearly makes her retch, but she continues to gasp in great gulps of air anyway.

Being pulled out to sea, further from the shore than Brenna, is the waif, the top half, her almost-human torso and face. The setting sun hits her in the face and it looks like she's melting, like a soap sculpture in an oven; she's dissolving into pink and yellow foam, her slick wet upper body is losing its details—her arms stick out, weirdly unbending—they appear to be reaching out to Brenna, as the waif's mouth opens and closes, working without purpose. She's drifting out faster than seems natural. Then the sea swallows her down. All that's left is this slick of sickly foam upon the surface of the water, mostly brown but with streaks of yellow and pink. All of it slowly mixing and diffusing.

Brenna stands up straight. The water comes to her lips. It was reckless to trust the King to keep his word, perhaps, when she can imagine how badly he would like to drink her down to the lowest fathoms, now that she's the victor. By his standards, anyway. But she intuited that his word would bind him. They aren't like humans, creatures such as the King and the Hag; they aren't mere sacks of meat and teeth that use words to get the things they want, any words at all. The creatures that have been speaking in her mind are in some more fundamental way made out of words, and thoughts, and dreams, and so must be more cautious with them. A vow of the Undersea King is part of his essence, and it might be suicide for him not to respect it as such.

The King figured that Mark and the waif made love, so they must be in love. He didn't get it that a human is free to do something, without it necessarily having anything to do with how they feel or what's inside them.

All this strange knowledge is already growing fuzzy and slippery in her head. There is nothing fuzzy about her memory of the waif's final transformation, though. Nor, she sees as she turns to the beach, about the destruction of George's and Albert's house. Neighbors are outside gawking, the crowd growing.

Mark is running into the surf in his underwear. He looks unharmed—he must have gotten out before the house collapsed. "Brenna!" Reaching her, he throws his arms around her. She returns the embrace, but can't really give herself over to it yet.

He leans back to look at her. "You're bleeding," he says, concerned.

Brenna only nods. That sounds about right, though she has no idea where on her body she's bleeding from. Every spot feels like an equally likely candidate.

He feels her distance. "Are you okay?"

"I'm fine."

Although it's kind of a selfish question under the circumstances, he can't help himself: "Are *we* okay?" He says, "I love you, Brenna. Do you still love me?"

"Yeah, man, I still love you, but just give me a minute." Something occurs to her, and she begins walking to the shore as fast as she can, pulling Mark after her as she works her way through the water. "Come on," she says, trying to keep her voice calm, but Mark can hear the urgency in it.

He doesn't question that urgency. He doesn't know exactly what happened, but he saw the monster that Pearl became chase Brenna into the sea before melting into foam, and frankly he'd like to get the hell out of the water too. Now that he's confirmed that Brenna is safe, he can't stop thinking about what this oily foul foamy slick is that they're walking through.

But then Brenna says, "And you'll have to get a new job. You can't be a lifeguard anymore."

"What?"

Brenna is ahead of him, pulling him after her by the arm. As their feet finally leave the water and slap onto the wet sand, she turns to Mark and hisses, "The Undersea King swore he wouldn't kill me in the water. He didn't say anything about *you*."

They walk to the wreckage of the house, Brenna's limp slowing them down. The noise of the surf is always there, in the back of everything, but the sounds of approaching sirens are beginning to rival it.

MISSION TO GWAPHARD

By the time the Wizards' mercenaries ambushed them in the clearing, Erewan and Lambrin had been traveling four days—hard going for Erewan, who, as a courtly lady (albeit in a minor court), was not used to it. For Lambrin, such journeys had been routine during his days as a wandering minstrel; anyhow, no journey was very hard, now that he was incorporeal. Had Erewan been on her own, she would have been hacked to pieces. But Lambrin was there to advise her, giving her the aid of his new Sight; moreover, she had the adrenal strength of her fury. She was dressed in little more than rags (though her boots were good), and she had removed her jewelry, and was traveling on foot like a peasant. The mercenaries could not have been seeking money, nor could they have deemed her a threat to their Master. Yet their first blows were killing ones, barely parried by her sword; had they wanted her body and her honor, she could have at least understood. But flesh they were so keen to destroy could not be their aim. She realized that pure bloodlust motivated them, and with a shout thrust as hard as she could.

Invisible Lambrin whispered instructions urgently in her ear: "Raise your sword to parry the big one, he's about to bring his blade down on your head!" The "big one," she sensed, was the one with the vicious spike jutting from his helmet, face and beard already splattered with dried blood, teeth ritually filed. His sword-stroke happened just the way Lambrin had said it would. "Jab, now, just to the left of where his left armpit is!" She obeyed, and, by the time she'd completed the motion, the big mercenary had stepped into exactly the right spot to receive her sword-point. He fell away, howling. Erewan's sword had drawn blood for the first time.

The wounded man's two companions were screaming their rage now, their eyes full of murder as they came at her. "Drop to your knees and slash across! Slice at the same level as Chanji's head!" Chanji was Lambrin's niece, well-loved enough by Erewan that the lady knew precisely how tall the child stood. As it turned out, that was exactly as high from the ground as the small gap underneath the heavy mail shirts of both her foes. The sword went deeper this time.

Lambrin did not let down his guard. "Now! Raise your sword! Jab up and back, behind your head!" She did, and felt her sword connect with something and hot blood spray her back and shoulders. The one behind her seemed to have had no armor. Perhaps he had been too poor. Trembling, now that there was time for it, Erewan stood. Two of the men yet lived; they writhed and moaned and burbled faintly. One was the bloody spike-hatted mercenary.

Erewan took shuddering breaths and stared at her gory handiwork. Even with Lambrin's help, had she really done all this? Could her lover have somehow guided the blade, even in his bodiless state?

"Ho!" The cry filled the clearing, booming through the emerald trees, echoing up to the bright sapphire sky, the voice seeming by some magical quality to carry power and authority within it.

"That's him," Lambrin murmured, sounding no less frightened than he had during the fray, "that's Gwaphard, the Wizard of Minlock Kingdom."

Erewan felt her knees nearly buckle. "Our Wizard," she whispered. Her eyes scoured the hillside above, and for a moment she thought that now, after four days' journey and a lifetime of stories, she would not see the Guardian Wizard after

all; perhaps he had cast a spell of invisibility over himself....
But, no, there he was, stepping out from the foliage onto an
outcropping of rock, a man of middle years, a brown beard of
middle length streaked with gray, wearing a loose brown robe
tied with a rope, his fists sternly on his hips, squinting down
suspiciously at them. "That's magic, isn't it?" he shouted, to be
heard across the distance. "You've got a ghost with you!"

"Half a ghost, sir!" called Lambrin.

The Wizard nodded impatiently: "Yes, yes, I can see that,
you're very faint." Erewan was startled—she, so far, had been
the only one able to hear her dead lover, but even she was not
able to see him. Maybe the Wizard Gwaphard would grant
her that boon, would allow her to see that beloved form once
more?... But she restrained herself. Wizards were notoriously
unsympathetic to and impatient with the desires of humans,
and it would be inviting his displeasure to make too many
requests. "I warn you," called the Wizard, "you should clear
out unless you want to both become ghosts, if that. There are
grave dealings afoot here."

She found then the courage to speak. "Sir," she cried up to
him, "all know of the Wizards' War which has occupied your
kind since before even my mother's birth—"

"Occupied!" the Wizard shouted back down, affronted.
"Occupied! Can you feeble humans even begin to grasp the
stakes for which we wage War? Before even your mother's
birth! For longer than that, I should say! What is a mere human
span, by our reckoning?"

Erewan could sense Lambrin's anxiety, and imagined
his phantom tugging at its hair and hopping from foot to
foot. Waiting courteously until she was sure Gwaphard had
finished, she continued: "Sir, it is true that neither I nor any
human I have ever met can say the causes of the Wizards' War.
As you know, of Wizards' affairs our knowledge is pitifully small.
But, sir, I was raised to know the laws that govern the dealings
of Wizards and humans. And so I know, sir, that, since we are
of the land of Tintian, and since you are the Wizard of Minlock

which encompasses that land, we are entitled to ask of you one boon, and you are bound to grant it, if you honorably can."

She had been frightened by her own boldness, and now she saw fury in the Wizards' grim face. "Yes, you humans have short memories for all but that!" he railed, "a compact made in the distant mists of the past, before even I, Gwaphard, can remember! For more millenia than you can imagine have I been troubled, pestered with humanity's every whim and whine, every sad and pathetic wish an impotent race can imagine!" He drew himself up: "No. Begone! I am a General, commanding legions of the Immortal, on the eve of a great Battle, and I have no time for such as you. Begone!"

The old woman Bijin, who had been her wet nurse, had warned her of this as she had secretly helped Erewan pack. The Wizards, the toothless crone had said, were imperious as infants, who could rule a household without ever doing anything for anybody. Gwaphard would no doubt refuse at first, but it would be a bluff—no matter what he might say, he was bound to the old laws the same way autumn leaves were bound to fall; as this was the price of the leaves' great beauty, that was the price of his great power.

Erewan, however, was in no mood to test old Bijin's claims. There was too much at stake. Before Gwaphard could withdraw back into the brush, she called, "I bring payment!"

Beside her, she could feel Lambrin bristle with disapproval, thinking she had made the offer too soon. Gwaphard hesitated. Trying to hide his interest behind a sneer, he said, "What could you possibly have with which to pay me?"

It had been too valuable to put in the sack. Reaching down the neckline of her tunic, she pulled out the small pouch that hung around her neck, and raised it for Gwaphard to see. "The Amulet of Tintian," she announced, "by the authority of which my family has ruled that humble land for two hundred years. The Amulet, too, is humble, yet I have heard that you can extract some power from it, if only a member of my family gives it willingly."

Gwaphard stroked his beard thoughtfully. "It would indeed be worth a little something," he mused; then, more loudly, "You know, girl, that if you relinquish the Amulet, your family's fortune will wither away. It is not a mere symbol, that. To give it up will surely spell the end of your family's reign in Tintian, and quickly."

Erewan stared back defiantly. "If it is in your power and will to grant my boon," she declared, "I will make any sacrifice."

Gwaphard shrugged. "Come up, then," he said, suddenly mild, and withdrew back into the brush.

Lambrin had already found the path up the mountain—or maybe, in his ghost state, with its heightened senses and awareness, "found" was not the right word. As Erewan was approaching it, though, he said to her, "Wait."

She paused. "What is it?"

"Aren't you forgetting something unfinished?" he asked.

Even then, for a moment, she had no idea what he meant; then, unwilling and horrified, she felt her attention drawn back to the two groaning, wounded men. "Oh, no...."

"You must, Erewan. I cannot hold a sword."

"No! Their comrades may yet find and tend them!"

"My love, I have some small bit of Sight now. Believe me, if you do not end their suffering, they will slowly writhe there all night, in agony, until finally death comes tomorrow."

Erewan squeezed her eyes shut a moment. Then she marched back to the wounded men and curtly cut their throats. Marching back to the path, and past Lambrin, she muttered, "Never speak of it."

He had no trouble finding a different subject. As they started up the hill, Erewan occasionally pausing to push some branches out of the way, or step around a massive root, or disentangle her foot from some vines, he murmured, "You shouldn't have told him about the Amulet, my love. He is bound by the old laws to help us, with or without reward. Now he won't be satisfied until he has it."

"We agreed that we were willing to part with it."

"Only after all else had failed."

"I don't care. I'll give him anything, if he will only help."

"But now your father will be ruined. He'll lose his dukedom, and know why, and that it was due to you. And he will disown you, and never forgive you. He may even come hunting you. And all of it will be because of me."

Erewan kept her lips sealed, and continued to climb. She thought of the Tintian of her childhood—of her whole life, until four days ago—laid waste by marauders. But she also thought of the exchange she and Lambrin had had the night before last, on the starlit Gray River Plain, just before she drifted off to sleep, as his sleepless soul stood watch over her; knowing that he could never lie to her, not now that he was a spirit, and thinking of the marvelous new Sight he had gained in exchange for his body, she had asked him, "My love, you died a week ago today, from eating bad mushrooms?"

"Yes," he had said. Already, she had been able to hear a strange, unfamiliar reticence in his tone.

"But you have been mushroom-gathering in the fields of Tintian a thousand times. And is it not true that you lived alone, off the land, from the end of your apprenticeship until you entered the services of my father as court minstrel?"

Lambrin cleared his throat. Erewan was astounded that a spirit should be able to do such a thing. "Mm," he said, "well, yes, that's true."

"So surely you must know the mushrooms of the forest well. Which are safe to eat, and which are deadly."

There was no reply from Lambrin. He hovered there, sullen and invisible.

"My love. Did you pick the mushroom which killed you?"

No answer had been forthcoming. She had pressed the question: "Did my father kill you, beloved?"

Now his tone had grown angry and distressed. "Be quiet," he'd commanded. "Go to sleep, and stop distracting yourself with such stupid musings." There had been something near tears in his voice, so she'd done as he'd said. As she'd rolled onto her side, though, she had silently decided that, no matter what else happened, the Amulet would never return to Tintian.

She pulled herself back to the here and now. It was no small thing to confer with a Wizard; not for lower nobility like her, anyway. The old folks said that once, back before the beginning of the Wizards' War, it had been easier. Nowadays, though, she might as well be a peasant. She summoned up all her courage and poise.

Suddenly, the Wizard was before them. Erewan squealed in shock, and then burned red with shame, even though she had also heard Lambrin gasp. Gwaphard looked amused, and his eyes flickered back and forth from Erewan to the empty space to her right. He said, "How does it feel, seeing your woman without her scent and paint, covered in sweat, bleeding from her scratches and cuts, perspiration soaking her beggar's rags, while you stand there, as much a dandy as you were the moment you died?"

"I feel proud of her, and ashamed of myself," said Lambrin. Erewan half-smiled, remembering his appearance— "dandified" was not altogether inapt—and wishing again that she could see him.

Gwaphard shrugged. "To business," he said roughly. "What have you come to ask me? And I warn you, it had better not be the life of your lover."

"No, sir," Erewan assured him; "only, we ask that he be allowed to continue to exist like this. My beloved knows a little—a very little—of the arts in which you are so adept, and so he has just managed to keep his soul coherent, and to hang by his fingertips over the void. It is not much, perhaps; still, he is able to exist, and we are able to love. But my father has hired exorcists to send my beloved's soul into oblivion. Mere hags, sir, old witches-of-the-lake, naked old ladies who share my puny mortal span, blind women who roll like pigs in the mud of the marsh, who chant their spells while gumming old roots and the corpses of salamanders. Sir, it would be less than nothing for you, in your great power, to smash their hag-spells out of existence, would it not? And then my love could continue to exist. Incorporeal as he is, he would still be able to stand over my bed at night, and whisper into my ear the simple love-secrets that keep me from the void, myself."

Throughout her appeal, the Wizard had never stopped eyeing them shrewdly. Now he said, "Is your father the Duke simply afraid of ghosts, or does he have some special quarrel with our spectral friend?"

"My father the Duke felt that my lover's rank made him unsuitable for me."

Gwaphard smirked, and scrutinized the spot where Lambrin must have been, all the while stroking his beard. "So you have some small knowledge of magic, do you?" he mused. "Hm. Your name is Lambrin. You were ... ah. Yes. You were Gardhee's Wizard's Apprentice, were you not?"

"Yes," said Lambrin. He did not sound proud—the word had the feeling of a confession.

"And he expelled you?"

Although Erewan had known of his expulsion, and had known that Gwaphard might mention it, her heart nevertheless stopped. For the second time, Lambrin the ghost cleared his throat. "Yes," he said, "but, I feel, unjustly."

Gwaphard's features were inscrutable. "I fought and vanquished Gardhee last year," he said.

Now Lambrin's voice lifted, with hope and, almost, joy. "Then ... maybe you understand...."

"Still," Gwaphard interrupted, "it is no small thing, being turned out by a Wizard, no matter which one. No other Wizard can overlook such a thing." Erewan's attention was drawn to the mysterious new psychic link between her and Lambrin, as she felt their hearts sink together. "Naturally, it is true that I could put an end to the meddling of some lake-hags with no effort at all. But the question is, what kind of soul would I be thus lending power to?"

Erewan spoke up: "But despite my beloved's youthful indiscretions, I will vouch for the goodness of his soul. And in any case, how can it hurt to merely save him from oblivion? He still will have no corporeal existence, and his knowledge of magic is far too feeble to cause any mischief."

Gwaphard wore a long-suffering expression. "But there is the matter of his just desserts."

"His desserts!" Erewan's indignation overcame her discretion; and then, in a fit of inspiration, she exclaimed, "I have heard tell of Hargwap, who preceded you as Wizard of Minlock Kingdom; Hargwap the Immortal, who lives on now as an omnipresent spirit; of whom it is said he can discern the secrets of any mortal soul. And I have also heard, sir, that he and you were the closest of companions, more brothers than master and pupil. Could you not summon him, sir, and ask him to tell you what he thinks of my beloved's desserts?"

For whatever reason, she had said the wrong thing. The Wizard's face crumpled and distorted itself in anger and something that looked like, had he not been a Wizard, grief. "Hargwap!" he exclaimed. "Girl, you would have me disturb the geat Hargwap? Hargwap, who has fought by my side in a thousand campaigns? Hargwap, who more than any other creature deserved the Immortal spark?" Gwaphard shook his head firmly, and declared, "No, he shall not appear, and you shall not have your foolish boon—not from me."

Lambrin's courage broke, and he let loose a despairing wail. Fighting for the strength to speak, she pleaded, "But he shall surely be gone by morning, he fades so quickly!"

Gwaphard spat on the ground. "Then let him go the natural way of all your kind."

Erewan's hands trembled. "But you only need stop the meddling of lake-hags, not extend his life yourself! And the law binds you to grant one boon of mine, if it be in your power!"

"And if I can do so honorably. How can I honorably help one whom another Wizard saw fit to cast out? No, no."

Erewan had not cried since childhood. Even a few days ago, when Lambrin's death had still been fresh, and she had not yet known he still existed at all, she had managed to remain collected. Now, though, tears of rage and furious grief sprang to her eyes, and she could hear Lambrin putting aside his own troubles to coo in her ear and console her, which only made her cry harder. "What is the use of greatness and power," she demanded of Gwaphard, "in the hands of a doddering old arrogant fool?!"

He behaved as if her censure were beneath his notice. Holding out his hand, he looked with a serious expression into her eyes. "As for the Amulet," he said softly, "name some other boon."

A wet, choking sound escaped her throat. For a moment, she stared helplessly at Gwaphard, wondering what to do. Then she took the Amulet out of its pouch and, too fast for anyone to stop her, dashed the crystal down onto a rock where it shattered, and ground the shards under her boot-heel. Her family's rank had shattered their love—so let her love shatter the family's rank!

If nothing else, she had managed to hurt the proud Wizard who had so casually defied the ancient bond. His eyes literally burned red for a moment—magic—as he struggled to regain control of his breathing. "Stupid child," he gasped. "You've destroyed your family and gained nothing for anybody."

"There was only one thing I wanted," she muttered bitterly.

Gwaphard gritted his teeth and stared at her, hard. She knew that he was tempted to kill her. In the end, though, he said, "You need no curse from me. In a few hours' time, your 'beloved' will lose his tenuous grasp on existence, and enter the maelstrom. And you have already murdered your father—he shall be dead by next sunrise." Something pierced her heart. The Wizard made a strange sign in her direction. "Fortune is ready to serve you the dish of ashes she has prepared. As for me, there is a battle looming in the valley below, and I have no more time to play with foolish mortals."

So saying, he withdrew into the foliage, and disappeared from view so quickly that Erewan knew it could not have been natural.

They were left alone in the bright clearing. Erewan could sense that Lambrin, beside her, was struggling to control himself in the face of such a monstrous disappointment. It wasn't easy for her, either. To take their minds off of inexorable doom, she said, "Let's climb," trying to put some cheerfulness in her voice, cheerfulness which sound like mockery in her own ears. Even so, she persevered. "Let's go up the hillside until we can find a place where we can watch the Wizards battle."

"Why," said Lambrin, the word falling like an anvil.

Despite her best efforts, Erewan could not smile. The best she could manage was to not scream and shred the flesh of her face with her nails. "Because I imagine it will be spectacular," she said, with a flat tone. "Because many people—most people—pass through whole lifetimes and never see—never dream of seeing—a battle of the Wizards' War."

"Very well," he muttered. His words were almost too quiet to be heard. She began to climb, hoping he would follow. He did. He made no sound, his sweet, invisible body melted through the twigs and brambles; but Erewan could feel him near. She did not speak because any word would be dangerous. Nothing, no remark, no matter how innocent, could be unrelated to Lambrin's impending second death, to the dissolution awaiting him, this very night. He lacked her will to silence, though. "The Wizard broke the law," he said, his voice high and dangerously near a loss of honor. "He lied, he slandered me, he claimed I was dishonorable. He didn't even bother to find the truth! You," and his voice lowered but at the same time acquired more intensity, "you must avenge me, Erewan, my love."

Erewan did not turn as she climbed, but kept her eyes straight. The slope was growing steeper. "The Wizard did lie indeed, and slander you, beloved," she said; "but I think perhaps he did not break the law."

Lambrin sounded bewildered and irritated: "What do you mean?" he demanded.

"I believe he lied from shame, not laziness." Amazing even to her, how her voice remained steady and unchanged. "I think the lake-hags have fooled my father, taken his money and the credit for an inevitable process. And the Wizard knew that, had I known this, had I known that the problem was not the witches-of-the-lake but the weakness of your own spell, then I would have asked him to grant you the secret of Immortality. And he was too proud to admit that this was beyond his power."

"But the Wizards do have the secret of Immortality, you stupid wench! What of Hargwap the Immortal?!"

Anger seeped in at the edges of her words. "I think he is dead," she bit off. "I think he fell in battle. I think the Wizards throw their lives away as foolishly as any human. Gwaphard, too, will pass. After his body has decayed, perhaps his spirit will cling to Earth a bit more tenaciously than yours can. But it, too, will fade."

It was as if she had told Lambrin news more devastating than his own death: "Why do you speak such heresies!" he wailed. "Is it not enough that my soul must wink out? You would destroy the universe to comfort me!" Erewan clamped her mouth shut, fearful of doing more harm. Lambrin, too, fell silent.

They continued to climb as the light waned. The hillside was, in fact, a mountainside, and they gained a respectable height. Pausing to rest in a clearing, they turned to look behind them and found that they had a majestic view of the valley below, and the untold thousands of Wizards who had massed there, two opposing forces facing each other. Without consulting Lambrin, Erewan sat on the steep green slope and watched the valley as if it were a stage. She felt him settle over her shoulder, felt him look in the same direction; but his soul was not quiet. Erewan did not speak, remembering that when she had, she'd only sharpened his sufferings.

As dusk approached, the Wizards began to stir. They did not fight as humans did—the troops, if that was the right word, were in no tight formations, seemed indeed to be milling about with the others of their side. Whatever they were doing was mostly too subtle for human senses; but it manifested itself in part as huge balls of light slowly volleyed back and forth from one side of the valley to the other, sometimes bursting silently high in the air above. The softly-glowing light balls seemed to grow larger as the battle went on; it was hard for the humans to be sure of anything, though, because the vision of the lights lulled them into something near a trance.

Lambrin began to make a high keening noise. "It's my last night of life, and you won't talk to me, talk to me!"

Erewan knew he was right. But she was exhausted and numb, and more talk could only bring pain. "What should I say, my love?" she asked, in a voice already resigned to not speaking.

"I don't know!" he wailed.

Terror was destroying the man she loved before he died. She took a deep breath, held it, released it, her eyes closed. "Lambrin, comfort me," she whispered.

That startled Lambrin back into control of himself. He grew more still, and closer to her. They watched the Wizards battle. It was truly night now, and the lights had grown even more marvelous. The bursts were huge now, filling half the sky and turning the night into a multicolored day of red, green, blue, orange. They had no effect discernible to human eyes, but Erewan could feel, somehow, vaguely and mysteriously, that with each starburst there were mighty and terrible consequences for the Wizards below, and she found herself grieving for them, grieving for foolish Gwaphard. Lambrin whispered that he loved her, and for the second time that day she was near tears. Then, suddenly, there was an especially magnificent display of lights, half a dozen huge multicolored fuzzy light balls exploding overhead one after the other, and this time with such intensity that, for the first time, they were audible, albeit barely; tiny little thwap, thwap noises. It was so unexpected and beautiful that she nearly clapped her hands in delight, and turned grinning to look over her shoulder and ask Lambrin if he had seen it. It was then she realized that he was gone.

TERRIBLE
TWO'S

"Daddy!" the twins squealed, as they stampeded into the foyer. Joe leaned over and gathered them into his massive arms, sending them into gales of hysteria by kissing their necks.

Carol smiled as she watched the children disappear into their father's bulk, the fingertips of one hand playing at her throat as she absently leaned her hip against the nineteenth-century end table. The sight warmed her heart. Sometimes she worried that Joe seemed distant from Timmy and Tina, especially considering that they were only two years old, nearly three.

But the memory of that warmth was burned away by panic when she got up to check on them in the middle of the night and found their room empty. She cried out to Joe, and together they searched the apartment. The toddlers weren't there. They called the police, the police showed up promptly, Carol and Joe answered the policemen's questions, and most of the officers departed, leaving behind a pair in case anyone called with a ransom demand. Even with the drama of a pair of abducted children to distract them, Carol noticed the police gazing appreciatively around their spacious Madison Avenue apartment.

Joe took Carol to sit apart from the officers, and plied her with white wine to try to calm her. She didn't want to be calmed. "How could this have happened?" she demanded. "How could someone come in and just steal them away?!"

"I don't know, Carol. Let's not concentrate on that right now."

"Do you think I left the front door unlocked?" she moaned, tormented by guilt. The front door had been unbolted. This was the third time Carol had asked Joe if she were responsible.

"No," he said again, still firm, still calm. "*I* locked it, and checked it again before bed, after we'd tucked in the twins."

Carol wanted to ask again how, in that case, it had gotten unlocked. But she was exhausted by the hysteria simmering just below the surface of her mind, plus the wine was taking its toll, and she drifted unwillingly into unconsciousness.

She awoke to Joe's gentle but irresistible hand hand shaking her shoulder. Before she could manage to open her eyes all the way, before she understood for certain that it was no mere nightmare that her children were missing, Joe said, "They've found the twins."

The last wisps of sleep were vaporized, and Carol sat bolt upright. "Where?! Are they all right?!"

"They're fine," he assured her. Then, cocking his head as if at a curious detail, he added, "The people who took them don't seem to be doing too well, though."

Tina and Timmy had been found in a couple's apartment in Brooklyn, covered in blood. Not their own. Their captors' throats had been cut, and the man also had a stab wound to the eye. Both victims had first been brought down to the floor by stabs to their ankle tendons. It really seemed that the toddlers had done it—the angles matched, as well as the low level of physical force. The cuts to the throats weren't all that deep, but they had managed to hit the jugulars dead on. The twins' prints were on the knives. Even before the prints were analyzed, anyone could see by the size that they were from children.

The toddlers were tearless, and seemed generally untraumatized. "They're probably in shock," the Social Services woman said to Carol. "Does your family watch a lot of violent movies?" she added, frowning at her with definite suspicion.

"No, we do not. No more than any other family. Anyway, these people kidnapped them! Is it unhealthy for them to defend themselves, just because they're children?" She was concentrating on the undeniable fact that it was good that the toddlers had killed those abducting child molesters, and trying not to think of anything else.

The children were able to explain basically what had happened. They had always been precocious; Carol suspected that Joe had been the same way. The children claimed to have no memory of leaving their home, but to have woken up at the Brooklyn apartment. There, the two residents had tried to touch Timmy "in a bad place," and Tina had grabbed a sharp knife that had been left on the coffee table and had jabbed both adults in the backs of the ankles. Timmy had grabbed a second knife, and together he and his sister had dispatched the pair. The children weren't able to explain what all these knives were doing laying around. Being mere children, they had thought nothing of it.

"Pretty resourceful," murmured Joe, watching his children closely, as if trying to gauge their movements and judge how their coordination measured up against other two-going-on-three-year-olds.

"Well, thank God they're resourceful," said Carol. "Now, Joe, I do not want them being made to feel like freaks!"

Joe asked the investigating officer if he could get copies of the files, but when the officer was reticent he dropped it for the moment. No need to reveal his high clearance to the policeman. He could always get copies of the files when he went to the office tomorrow, at the Organization.

Carol felt as if she would never be able to bring her mind near this ordeal without feeling the sickness of its rancid horror leaking into the whole of their lives. A thing like this could not help but poison the life of a family, no matter whether everyone on Earth agreed that the twins had not done anything wrong and could not be held responsible even if they had.

Family life was already a stressor for Carol, though it made her feel guilty to admit it. She had never quite felt secure with

Joe—not in the sense that she was afraid of him, exactly, but that she worried he might leave her someday. Not for another woman; it simply seemed at times that all merely human relations were outside his primary scope of interest. And yet she clung to him. She was afraid of being alone. When they'd gotten married, and then more when she'd gotten pregnant, she'd told herself that all such doubts were bound to end. And the bond between the four of them had indeed seemed strong, for the most part. But what with this macabre tragedy, her old insecurities returned to the surface.

Just when she was beginning to think they would all move on with their lives, a horrible visitor appeared.

Joe was at work, at the Organization. It had been so long since Carol had learned not to question her husband about his work, that she forgot to be curious about it herself. The twins were at a Disney movie with Carol's parents. She had been planning to accompany them—she could hardly bear to let the children out of her sight, now more than ever—but both her husband and her parents had insisted that she looked tired and needed an afternoon off. She was sitting in the living room with some Chopin playing, sipping at white wine and furiously willing herself to relax, when she heard a popping noise, followed by the sound of the door opening.

Carol gave an involuntary little shriek at the noise. Figuring the intruder had already heard her and knew she was there, she dashed from her bedroom into the kitchen. Along the way she caught a glimpse of a short wild-haired man flailing through the living room, like a troll or an electrocuted clown. He spotted her, shouted something. In the kitchen she dove for the knife rack—she yanked a big knife out of the rack and spun around, holding the blade between her and the hallway. She patted her pocket and realized that her phone wasn't there—then, with a sob of relief, she saw she'd left it right there on the kitchen counter.

By the time the intruder flung himself against the doorframe she had already dialed 911, and had the phone to her ear. "Are you calling the police? Wait, don't!" he cried. He was a short, unimpressive man in rumpled clothes, and might not have been so scary if not for the half-mad harried look on his unshaven face, his wild hair in a crazy halo behind the bald front half of his scalp. Also the thing he was waving in his right hand, which she guessed was the tool he'd used to jimmy her lock. It was not an icepick, but looked like it could be used as one. He seemed only now to notice it himself, and lowered it a bit (but not completely), as he held his left hand out to her beseechingly, saying, "Please! Just try to stay calm!," which was not very convincing given how nearly panicked he himself sounded.

The operator picked up and asked what her emergency was.

"Hello, I have an intruder in my apartment!"

"Lady, you don't need to call the police! Look, we can just talk...."

"Yes, he's right here. He's waving an icepick at me!"

Hearing this, the intruder lowered the icepick-thingie more, but immediately raised it again as if he couldn't bear to be without it. He continued to beg her not to bring the police into this even as she was giving them her address.

Suddenly the phone went dead. Carol couldn't believe it. "Shit!" she said, and slammed the phone back on the counter, keeping the knife trained on the intruder.

His eyes got even stranger as he said, "Did the line go dead?"

Now Carol realized that it would have been smarter to have pretended to still be on the line with the police. "They know where we are! They're on their way."

"Whoever was listening in and cut the connection is on their way, too.... Listen, just keep calm. Okay? Let's just keep calm, and talk. I swear that I'm not here to hurt you. Just let me talk to you, okay?"

"All right, fine, talk."

"I just need your kids—"

"Get the fuck out of here! Get out of my apartment! How the hell did you get by the doorman, anyway?!"

"Calm down! Listen, I … ah, Jesus. Listen, I work with your husband. You know where your husband works?"

Carol had a moment's hesitation. She said, "I'm not allowed to talk about that."

"All right. Fine. I'll do the talking. You don't know this, but there are these particles, certain particles we've discovered, and they can go back in time, and at the Organization we've been working on the idea that maybe they can transmit information from the future. Okay? And, well, it turns out they can. We received two discrete communications. Whoever sent them knew exactly how to direct them to our apparatus, which makes sense, because they're in the future, and we're in the past, so they, I don't know, they could just go through the Organization's old records, I guess. That stuff probably isn't even fucking classified anymore, where they are.

"Now, like I said, our computers received two discrete communications, at practically the same time. They were both very different—one was almost like a, a *hail*, a hand waving to get our attention, but the other one slipped into our computers the back way. Even though the programs and receptors are designed to look for messages, this one was so subtle that if we hadn't been alerted by the first one, the hail, to go look for it, it might never have been detected.

"That first message, the loud one, consisted of three parts: first the big *hello!* at the front, then a tutorial explaining how to read this type of message. That was pretty complicated. It took a day, and we had some pretty smart guys working on it—about the smartest money can buy.

"Then the third part told us what the second, camouflaged message was doing.

"See, it turns out that in the future the Earth has been invaded by aliens...." At this Carol, still holding the knife, made a funny noise, and the intruder responded with a pleading look, appealing to her to hear him out. He said, "It's been invaded by aliens, but there's a human resistance movement, and it shows no sign of being outright defeated anytime soon—I mean, it *will* show no sign of being defeated anytime soon *then*, I mean what's soon for them but is still far away for *us*...."

"Please leave," said Carol.

"No, come on, wait. So the aliens hacked backwards in time into the Organization computer and installed a new program. We're right at the limit of how far back in time you can send such messages, because we at the Organization only just perfected the technology a few days ago. What the aliens sent back was a program that surreptitiously directs our machines to create nanobots out of molecules scavenged from Organization computers and dust. Then the nanobots attached themselves to someone leaving the office to go out in the world and build more complex machines, machines inside the brains of humans who would then become puppets. Those humans would find their victims, their victims being the ancestors of some of the most important leaders in the resistance movement's history. One such person was the husband in that couple that allegedly abducted your twins."

"What the hell do you mean, 'allegedly'? They came here and kidnapped them, didn't they?!"

"Your twins have no free will anymore. They're cyborg killers controlled by microcomputers the nanobots built at the centers of their brains."

"That doesn't make any sense! Why would they pick *children*?!"

"They couldn't pick someone at the Organization— we'd be watching our employees too close. So they attached to someone's clothes—your husband's clothes—and passed from there to your kids probably because they were the first people he touched. Luckily we caught on pretty quick to what was happening and have stopped letting anyone leave the compound without passing through a cyber scrubber that should scramble all electronics. Hopefully your husband was the only carrier.... As for why they picked children, well, you know—they're aliens. They get it that children are innocuous, but it didn't occur to them that they're conspicuous, too. They would have been smarter to have picked you."

"Shut up! Shut up, you psycho pervert!"

"Your husband would have figured all this out for himself, only he's in a different department and hasn't been cleared to know any of it. Once we'd deciphered the resistance movement's message, and as soon as I heard that crazy story about your kids, I told my bosses, 'We've got to dispatch those kids now! Those computers in their heads could be making more nanobots as we speak!' But those bureaucrats might take a whole day to do anything. We can't risk that much time."

"What did you mean, 'dispatch'?"

"Lady, it would be a mercy to them. Look, I'm sorry if you won't listen to reason, but tell me where are your kids?"

"Not here, asshole! At a movie with my parents!"

The intruder cursed, and said, "What theater?"

Carol realized that the intruder was dead-set on killing her children, and it suddenly seemed reckless to depend on the police being able to keep them safe. She lunged at him with the knife—he ducked out of the way and tried to grab the arm of her knife hand but missed. She took a swipe at him which nearly slashed his throat, but then her next swing hit the doorway to the kitchen and the knife clattered to the floor. He grabbed her then. To his credit, he seemed to have no interest in stabbing her with the icepick-thingie—apparently that was only for opening the door, and killing her kids. While they were struggling the police finally got there.

Only moments after the police had separated Carol and the intruder, Joe showed up, along with a grim-looking companion, a thin man in his late thirties with black hair and a thin nose. Joe came to her and encased her upper arm in his firm, gentle, strong hand. "Everything will be all right, Carol," he said.

She looked up at him, confused. "I thought you were at work?"

"We have ways of getting around quickly."

As far as Carol knew, Joe's branch of the Organization was

about an hour into New Jersey. But who knew? Maybe they had secret supersonic subterranean trains, or something.

Meanwhile, the thin man had taken one of the policemen aside and shown him his badge. The officer, sounding confused and almost a little bit frightened, said, "Is … is that real?" After some murmured discussion between the police, Joe, and the thin man, and some radioing back to the precinct, it was decided that the police would escort Carol someplace quiet while Joe and his work friend spoke to the intruder.

"But why do *I* have to go?!" asked Carol, as the policemen were ushering her out. "*He's* the one who broke in!"

Joe came to stand close and comfort her. "Honey, we have to have a private conversation with this man. I'm sorry I can't explain, but it's a matter of national security. You know that trumps everything else."

She did. As she allowed the cops to gently nudge her out the door, she saw that the intruder seemed relieved as he whispered to Joe and his companion, like he'd expected them to be angry but instead found them quite reasonable.

It was embarrassing, walking through the lobby with the police. She wanted to explain to the doorman that she wasn't the one being arrested, but didn't. The police took her to Starbucks and bought her a latte. She tried calling her parents a couple times but they probably had their phones off because they were still in the movie. After a while the police got an all-clear message on their radios and took her back to her apartment, where they left her. Joe wasn't there anymore. He'd left a note, though.

She kept calling her parents—she would have gone looking for them, except she didn't know what theater they were at. Finally her mother called to say that Joe had come to the theater while the movie was playing and had found the twins and their grandparents, explaining that something had happened and he needed to take the children. He'd had a couple of men with him. "Is everything okay?" asked Carol's mother.

"Oh, yes. I'll explain it all later."

"It's funny that he knew what theater we were at. I don't think we said where we were going. How did he know what theater we were at?"

Carol ducked the question. She was sure Joe had lots of ways of finding things like that out.

It was good that he had picked the children up. Now that the twins were with Joe, they would be safe.

But he didn't bring them straight home. That was odd. It seemed very odd that he didn't bring them straight home to her. Given the kind of day it had been, you would have thought he'd bring them straight home.

She sat in the twins' room for a while. Holding Tina's stuffed unicorn, she was horrified to find herself imagining innocent Timmy and Tina, appearing upon the surprised Brooklyn couple's doorstep, the couple trying to figure out who these children were and where they'd come from, one of the twins distracting the couple in the living room while the other pulled a chair over to the kitchen counter so he or she could reach the knife rack.... She shook her head sharply, feeling guilty for crediting the intruder's crazy story even in her imagination....

The intruder had said it should have been Carol that the nanobots picked. That was true, she thought, it should have been her.

Finally she heard the key in the lock. (The tool the intruder had used had not broken the lock—like it was designed to open doors stealthily.) She was sitting in the living room by then, trying to force herself to relax by drinking white wine—at the sound of Joe's return she sprang out of her seat and rushed to meet him, then stopped short. Staring at him, she said, "But where are the twins?"

Never had she seen him look so tired. He met her gaze, sighed, then turned and went into the kitchen, pulling his tie off as he went. The wine bottle was where she'd left it on the counter. He poured himself a glass.

She followed him into the kitchen. "But where are the children?"

He turned and faced her, leaning against the counter. Sipped at the wine, and said, "Carol. Remain calm, please."

"What? Where are they!"

"Normally this would all be top-secret, but considering what you've already heard I've received special permission to tell you that the twins each had a tiny computer at the centers of their brains."

"What? What? What were they doing there?"

"Our people are studying them now."

"Well, I don't care what they were for, as long as Timmy and Tina are okay! Are they? Are they okay?"

"The computers were placed right in the center of the brain, apparently built by nanobots from the inside, each about the size of a pea, with no way to remove it without destroying the surrounding brain."

"Without destroying the brain? But you said they were studying the computers, so they must have...."

She trailed off. He nursed his wine. Carol's eyes glazed over and she gazed into space.

Joe said, "It was a matter of the survival and triumph of the human race itself."

Carol didn't reply, because what could you say to something like that?

Then Joe said, "But, Carol, it's all right," and she looked up at him, gasping with hope and relief, realizing she'd misunderstood.

But he only said, "We can make more children. As many as you like."

Carol stared at him. Then she left the kitchen. The bathroom was a good place to be alone—she went there and shut the door behind her. Joe stayed in the kitchen nursing his wine. He let her be alone.

HOW I LOVE
HANNAH

Sex Machine was playing, James Brown's vigorous health mocking me as I chopped and diced the baby's arm on the cutting board in the kitchen. Years ago, the nature of my tasks had appalled and repulsed me. But, as time went on, my attitude became closer to that of someone ashamed to admit to his menial but necessary job; as if I were the man who puts down puppies at the pound. As I worked, my mind was more on Hannah than the blood. Would she be home on time? Would she be exhausted, would she have more work to do, would she be uncontrollably excited over something beyond my ability to comprehend? Or would we be able to finally have a quiet night at home?

Then, as I was finishing up, my eye wandered over to the pile of clothes that the corpse had come in. That Winnie the Pooh bib: the other day I'd gone to my sister's house, and her baby had been wearing a bib just like it. When I noticed the applesauce stain, my hands began to shake. Same bib. I looked back down at the bowl and the messy counter, unable to remember the face; it was mush now. After a while, you stop noticing faces. And you stop looking at the faces of live babies, too—even though I'd noticed the bib yesterday, I don't think I'd ever looked straight at my nephew's face for more than a second, during that one visit I'd paid my sister since his birth.

But the truth was obvious, and I sat down and lit a cigarette. Hannah didn't like it when I smoked inside, but she could go to hell. My hands were shaking so badly that I nearly burnt my nose getting the cigarette lit. Two puffs later, I realized that I had no ashtray, and I grabbed an unused bowl from the cupboard and sat back down.

In the early days, I'd resisted. Nothing heroic, but I could see that the work was disgusting and so I tried to fight. The futility of that had grown clear soon enough, and I'd compromised, settling down into the work, and life with Hannah. Which, surprisingly—the most pleasant surprise of my life—had turned out to be not so bad, for the most part. We'd had rocky times, especially when we were in the early stages of becoming a couple. Some dangerous times. But things worked out; I settled into my role as housekeeper, assistant, servant, familiar, and bedmate, until in recent years I'd become something closer to a partner (although my comprehension of the mysteries Hannah worked in remained laughable). She hardly used her binding spells at all anymore, not really. I dusted her tomes and straightened the broomsticks in the closet (Hannah never put them back neatly, she just flung them in there), and did other odd jobs.

I lit a new cigarette from the old one and thought about my sister, Jackie. The other day had been the first time I'd visited her in months, and we hadn't talked long. Jackie doesn't like talking to me much. For one thing, she knows there's something not quite right about me and my "girlfriend," Hannah. Anyway, she'd been rushed, since she had to get her oldest kid ready for a soccer game and herself ready for a PTA meeting. I didn't mind the lack of attention; I only stopped by because Hannah had instructed me to visit my family every so often, so that no one became suspicious of my absences and began prying into what went on in her house. I didn't stay longer than half an hour. Jackie had bumped into me as she was rushing down the hall and, still without looking at my face, muttered, "Oh, excuse me, Burt," before rushing on. We never had much to talk about. Still, it had been my sister's baby. It had been my own new nephew. The more I brooded over it, the harder my resolve grew. Like I said, she had grown more and more lax with the spells she had over me, as we'd grown closer. If she suspected nothing, then I would have a good chance. And I would take that chance. I would kill her.

Never mind whether it was the right thing to do, or not. True, Hannah killed babies, or rather had me kill them. But as I'd gone deeper into the world of witchery I'd come to realize the naiveté of labeling Hannah or her coven "evil." High-level witchcraft simply requires infant sacrifice—there's no getting around that, it's a fact of life. If Hannah's coven didn't keep itself strong, some other coven would muscle in. And, in the course of tagging along on Hannah's adventures, I'd seen enough to learn what a disaster that would be. Some of those crazy witches want to burn the world down. Literally. If one of the hard-line covens ever manages to take over, there might be no such thing as a human infant, ever again.

But to hell with it. She'd made me chop up my own nephew. I was going to kill her for that. Let someone smarter than me figure out whether it was ethical.

I may seem domesticated. But I have a rough past. When Hannah first met me I was a drunken brawler whose nose had been broken half a dozen times. It was back during those bad days that Jackie and the rest of my family had stopped wanting to be around me. If anything, Hannah's influence had made me more manageable.

The night I met her I'd gotten drunk alone at the Sizzler at the mall and was stumbling home through the suburban streets. Though the colored lights of televisions flickered through some of the houses' curtains, the streets were deserted.

Except for Hannah. Though I didn't know that was her name, and I certainly didn't know what she was—I didn't believe there were any such things as witches. But I could tell there was something about her. She stood on the edge of a neatly manicured lawn, her head back as she studied the stars.

I thought she was just looking at the stars because stars are a thing to look at. Of course, it was for a spell. Usually when a spell requires an invocation to the stars she has to go out to the countryside, but this time it was Venus she needed. Even from our neighborhood, Venus is visible.

I swaggered over to her. I guess I wanted to mess with her, at most scare her some. But when she kept her head tilted back as if she didn't see me, even though I was practically on top of her, it discombobulated me. And to hide the fact, I suppose I got more aggressive.

"Hey," I snapped. My alcoholic breath wafted along her outstretched neck. She still pretended not to notice me. Probably she couldn't acknowledge me without throwing off the stellar invocation, but I couldn't have known that then.

"Hey," I slurred again, more roughly. I reached for her wrist, and even through my drunken haze was surprised when she let me take it without yanking it back. "Hey. You shouldn't be out here alone. You know that? A babe like you. Something could happen."

And still she kept her gaze aloft. Now at last I began to feel uneasy—at the same time, I no longer had any choice but to get her attention. Otherwise it would have stuck in my craw the rest of my life.

Who knows what I would have done, if she hadn't finally looked down from the stars and into my eyes. I nearly took a step backwards, but managed to hold my ground and return her gaze. "What is it you want?" she said.

I was too drunk to think of a snappy comeback, so I just leered.

She smirked in response. "Is that all," she said disdainfully, then jerked her head to indicate the bushes in front of the house. "Will over there do?"

I stared at her. I was like the dog who caught the car and suddenly had to figure out how to drive it. But she still had that sneer pointed my way, and I couldn't let her get the better of me. So I said, "Yeah. Whatever."

She led me to the bushes. I wondered why we didn't just go inside, since I assumed this was her house (turned out it wasn't; her house—our house, now—is down the block).

Determined as I was not to crack before she did, just before I entered her I couldn't help but hesitate and say, probably in almost a frightened voice, "Hey … this is your idea, all right? So, you know, I'm not doing anything wrong."

She only lay there, looking up at me impassively. Sizing me up. I had to demonstrate that she hadn't thrown me off, that I wasn't bothered by her, that I could take her body with no second thoughts, without being unmanned by her face. So I pushed myself in.

I tried gloating. As if I were taking her, as if she'd found my strength irresistible or something. But I wasn't buying it and she definitely wasn't. I watched her face in the cold street light. She lay perfectly still and stared up at me with stern, implacable eyes, her mouth a tight line. I made myself finish, then rolled off of her. I was catching my breath, getting ready to continue on my way home, quieter now, when all of a sudden there were stripes and lashes of searing pain inside my chest, as the binding spell took hold. I lay gasping as Hannah cleaned herself with handfuls of grass, and said, "I served you for less than a minute. Very well. You'll repay me with service for the rest of your life, dog."

But, although there were many minor humiliations at the start, she never quite fulfilled her threat to treat me like a dog—and, as the months and then the years of easy servitude went on, I saw that she was at heart a gentle person, albeit one devoted to ruthless work. What began to occupy me more than her grisly tasks, was the way she let me give her back massages to knead the stress out; the way she once squealed when a champagne cork popped and went flying across the room, a squeal which surprised us both; the way she'd trembled in fear when the rest of the coven was displeased with her, and the way she'd allowed me to console her during that bad time. What mattered was that she made me her lover. Sometimes

I would wake up screaming, or beg her to set me free, or throw coffee cups against the wall, but for the most part I accepted her work's perversions. They were necessary, for a myriad of reasons: a few of which I understood, most of which I did not.

But now she had gone too far. To make me party to the murder of my own nephew! I lit yet another cigarette as I brooded and brooded, clenching my jaw hard enough to grind the enamel from my molars. The needle lifted itself from the finished LP, and the silence fell like snow upon the room. I watched the smoke tangle in the air. From the counter, I took the bloody knife and placed it on the kitchen table beside me. It was the one I usually used for my assignments, and Hannah would not think it strange to see it there. I smoked furiously and refused to think of the way her eyes grew heavy-lidded when she was tired. Instead, I dwelt on the bib, on my harried stranger-sister rushing out the door for her PTA meeting, on the cruel and biting and emasculating things that Hannah had occasionally said to me, and I tried to conjure up that old mad me, the one who had drank himself into blood-frenzies and gone marching off down peaceful streets in search of things to hurt.

I heard her unlock the door, open it, slam it. The house is medium-sized, a two-bedroom, and it only took a moment for her to step into the kitchen. Whatever she'd been doing, she'd had a bad day—she was pale, with faint purple circles under her eyes; the neat bun of her brown hair had come a little loose, and there were hair strands swaying like underwater plants. Her square face was tense.

Without looking me, she went straight to the sink to look at my handiwork, and, still without turning to face me, said, "You're in a mood, I guess."

"Oh yeah? What makes you think that?"

"You didn't put on a new record." She took a fork out of the cutlery drawer and used it to poke around the contents of the bowl, satisfying herself that I'd done the job competently. "When you're in good mood you listen to music. Something must be eating at you. You've been sitting there smoking like

138

a petulant boy, stinking up the house and composing a piece of your mind to give me." She leaned in closer to the bowl, examining a suspect chunk; then, having decided that it would pass muster, she continued, still without deigning to look at me: "Well, go on. Give it to me."

Defiantly, I lit yet another cigarette, even though I knew she could turn me into a roach for it, if she wanted. "The bib."

Her muscles tightened. Most people wouldn't have noticed. "Ah," she said. "I didn't think you would recognize the particular baby. But the bib ... it didn't even occur to me.... He was wearing it when you went to see Jackie?"

"Yeah. He was."

After a very long moment, which Hannah spent silently checking and double-checking the contents of the bowl, she said, "Sorry. But it was necessary."

"My own nephew," I said. "Why him? God, Hannah, I would have found you another baby! I would've gone out myself and found one!"

She'd gotten some blood on her jeans—"Damn," she said, standing back and looking down at them. Then she returned her attention to my handiwork. Bending down and getting a cookie sheet out of the pots-and-pans drawer, she set it on the stove beside the bowl and began placing the pieces on it, carefully following some system of organization that I didn't understand. "Had to be your nephew," she muttered.

I could tell she was sick of talking about it, and that only made me angrier and more determined to have it out. "Why?" I demanded. "Why him?"

"Part of the charm," she muttered, so quietly now that I could hardly hear her. "Charm says chopper chops his blood and bone. His own."

This deflated me a little; but I refused to give in, even if she'd had a valid reason. "You should have told me." I meant to say it accusingly, but it came out sullen.

Now she laughed, my least favorite of her laughs, a mirthless and contemptuous "Hah!," and turned to face me, leaning her butt against the edge of the counter with her hands on the countertop. "What good would that have done?" she demanded. "It wouldn't have changed anything. You still would have had to do the job. Would it have been easier if you'd known?"

"I would have refused."

"You would have refused. You would have refused, and then I would have had to bind you. But I don't want to use the binding spells on you, Burt. Not if I don't have to. I suppose that's selfish of me—I suppose it was, this time. But I didn't want to."

I kept my mouth shut. She turned back to the bowl and continued to lay the pieces out. "Anyway, you have no idea how important this charm will be. This potion will go on to be a very small but needed part of something that will be myth-fodder for millennia."

"I don't care."

"You don't care," she repeated, wearily now, her back still to me. Hannah doesn't react well when she thinks she owes someone an apology. "You don't care. Fine. Why don't you just sit there and not care quietly, huh, so that I can get on with my work?"

Red spots popped before my eyes and I felt pincers jabbing their way through my temples, from the inside out. Only then did I realize that I was really going to do it, I was going to slide the knife into her, I was going to pierce her there in the bloody kitchen. I reached out and grabbed the knife by the hilt. My haunches rose a millimeter off the chair as I prepared to pounce, to lunge.... Hannah reached back with her right hand, held the flesh under the nape of her neck, and pulled forward, stretching it. There was something kittenish in the gesture, and at the same time it reminded me of her weariness, of her hard labor, of the way she needed me. I fell feebly back into the chair, and let go of the knife.

Now Hannah turned to look at me, trembling. "Burt?" she said. Although she probably hadn't been monitoring her surveillance spells closely enough to have saved her life, if I'd gone through with it, they had tingled sufficiently to let her know that something was wrong. She looked at me in fear—not fear for her life, but for our love. "Burt?" she said. "Were you really going to?"

"No, baby," I murmured, and held out my arms. She climbed into my lap, and for a few moments I was the strong one and she the weak, as I took her brown hair out of the bun and stroked it and rubbed her back as she breathed into the hollow of my neck. I know that my sister would never forgive me if she knew what I'd done, and what I'd had the chance to do and didn't. But what can I say? I'm Hannah's, and she's mine. Thick and thin.

If you enjoyed this book, please help support it by rating it on Amazon, Goodreads, and any other online forum.

And we hope you'll go to saltimbanquebooks.com and sign up for our mailing list.

Thanks!

ABOUT THE AUTHOR

J. Boyett is a novelist, playwright, filmmaker, and founder of Saltimbanque Books, and can be reached at jboyettjboyett@gmail.com.

For more information check out jboyett.net.

ALSO FROM SALTIMBANQUE BOOKS:

BENJAMIN GOLDEN DEVILHORNS, by Doug Shields

A collection of stories set in a bizarre, almost believable universe: the lord of cockroaches breathes the same air as a genius teenage girl with a thing for criminals, a ruthless meat tycoon who hasn't figured out that secret gay affairs are best conducted out of town, and a telepathic bowling ball. Yes, the bowling ball breathes.

RICKY, by J. Boyett

Ricky's hoping to begin a new life upon his release from prison; but on his second day out, someone murders his sister. Determined to find her killer, but with no idea how to go about it, Ricky follows a dangerous path, led by clues that may only be in his mind.

BROTHEL, by J. Boyett

What to do for kicks if you live in a sleepy college town, and all you need to pass your courses is basic literacy? Well, you could keep up with all the popular TV shows. Or see how much alcohol you can drink without dying. Or spice things up with the occasional hump behind the bushes. And if that's not enough you could start a business....

THE VICTIM (AND OTHER SHORT PLAYS), by J. Boyett

In *The Victim,* April wants Grace to help her prosecute the guys who raped them years before. The only problem is, Grace doesn't remember things that way.... Also included: A young man picks up a strange woman in a bar, only to realize she's no stranger after all;

An uptight socialite learns some outrageous truths about her family;

A sister stumbles upon her brother's bizarre sexual rite;

A first date ends in grotesque revelations;

A love potion proves all too effective;

A lesbian wedding is complicated when it turns out one bride's brother used to date the other bride.

COMING IN SUMMER 2015:

COLD PLATE SPECIAL, by Rob Widdicombe

Jarvis Henders has finally hit the beige bottom of his beige life, his law-school dreams in shambles, and every bar singing to him to end his latest streak of sobriety. Instead of falling back off the wagon, he decides to go take his life back from the child molester who stole it. But his journey through the looking glass turns into an adventure where he's too busy trying to guess what will come at him next, to dwell on the ghosts of his past.

STEWART AND JEAN, by J. Boyett

A blind date between Stewart and Jean explodes into a confrontation from the past when Jean realizes that theirs is not a random meeting at all, but that Stewart is the brother of the man who once tried to rape her. Or is she the woman who murdered his brother? And will anyone ever know?

I'M YOUR MAN, by F. Sykes

It's New York in the 1990's, and every week for years Fred has cruised Port Authority for hustlers, living a double life, dreaming of the one perfect boy that he can really love. When he meets Adam, he wonders if he's found that perfect boy after all ... and even though Adam proves to be very imperfect, and very real, Fred's dream is strengthened to the point that he finds it difficult to awake.

THE UNKILLABLES, by J. Boyett

Gash-Eye already thought life was hard, as the Neanderthal slave to a band of Cro-Magnons. Then zombies attacked, wiping out nearly everyone she knows and separating her from the Jaw, her half-breed son. Now she fights to keep the last remnants of her former captors alive. Meanwhile, the Jaw and his father try to survive as they maneuver the zombie-infested landscape alongside time-travelers from thirty thousand years in the future.... Destined to become a classic in the literature of Zombies vs. Cavemen.